Sun Kissed Hearts

Stephanie Doering

Published by Stephanie Doering, 2025.

This is a work of fiction. Similarities to real people, places, or events are entirely coincidental.

SUN KISSED HEARTS

First edition. February 10, 2025.

Copyright © 2025 Stephanie Doering.

ISBN: 979-8230548171

Written by Stephanie Doering.

Table of Contents

Chapter 1: A New Beginning 1
Chapter 2: Unexpected Command 7
Chapter 3: Island Discoveries 13
Chapter 4: Unseen Connections 18
Chapter 5: Settling In 23
Chapter 6: Converging Paths 28
Chapter 7: A New Perspective 38
Chapter 8: The Secret Beach 46
Chapter 9: Sunset Encounters 53
Chapter 10: Shared Moments 60
Chapter 11: Leaving Paradise 66
Chapter 12: A New Vision 75
Chapter 13: Hidden Talents 81
Chapter 14: Shared Moments 87
Chapter 15: A New Dawn 94

To all my adored readers,

I hope you enjoy this. I know this is not necessarily something I write, but during the cold winter months I had this desire to write somethng of this magnitude and this is what that labor of love became. I hope you enjoy it as much as I did creating it.

Chapter 1: A New Beginning

At 22, she had her life mapped out for her. She planned to get her master's in photography and establish her career. Then, she would settle down and marry Daniel and maybe even start a family of her own. Now though, her meticulously planned life had been thrown into disarray. Daniel had broken up with her right before graduation shattering her dreams of a future together. To make matters worse, her professor had cast doubt on her abilities, making her question whether she was talented enough to pursue photography as a career.

Usually, she was not this adventurous but she needed the change in scenery so she decided to get away from the life she knew and take a month-long vacation to a tropical oasis.

She wasn't traveling to some well-known all-inclusive resort; rather was opting for a more rural locale. She was visiting an island reputed for its pink sands and crystal-clear blue waters, it also possessed a rich historical heritage and lush tropical jungles. Most importantly though, this was the vacation she needed to re-evaluate her life. The past few years had been a whirlwind of responsibilities and relentless routines. Now, she was ready to immerse herself in the serenity of nature, away from the noise and haste of her everyday existence. She hoped that the island's peaceful ambiance would provide her with the clarity she desperately needed to make some important decisions about her future.

This getaway was less about running away from her responsibilities and more about trying to figure out what her future looked like. She was the "good girl", the responsible child who didn't do anything wrong, unlike her older brother, Zephyr who at 28 didn't have a steady job, constantly had to borrow money from their parents, and had dropped out of college due to excessive drug and alcohol use, yet her parents didn't see it that way. No, her parents just believed that Zephyr hadn't found out what he enjoyed doing in life and felt that Elara was being too critical of her brother. It was a double standard she didn't quite understand.

At the same time, they did not understand why Elara wanted to travel alone to a foreign place when she had everything she needed at home. Elara felt frustrated that her parents believed she was too critical of her brother and considered her decision to take a vacation to reassess her life as irresponsible. She wanted them to understand that seeking some time away after her breakup with Daniel and the criticism she received from Professor Hayes before graduation was not an act of irresponsibility, but an act of self-evaluation.

Elara knew that explaining this to her parents was like trying to describe the color blue to someone blind. They saw her meticulously planned life, her acceptance into a promising career program, her consistent academic achievements, and her dedication to family as a sign of stability. They saw Zephyr's chaotic life as an adventure waiting to be discovered. They simply couldn't comprehend that the constant pressure to be the "good girl," coupled with recent personal setbacks, had finally taken their toll. This trip wasn't about abandoning everything she had strived for; it was about rebuilding the foundation for her own definition of success, a definition that went beyond pleasing others.

The hum of the jet engine vibrated through Elara's bones, a monotonous drone that mirrored the hollow feeling in her chest. She leaned back against the stiff headrest, the vibrant blues and greens of the travel magazine in her lap blurring into an indistinguishable mess. Isla del Sol, a mythical haven shimmering on the edge of her imagination, felt impossibly far away, not just geographically, but emotionally. The anticipation of the journey was overshadowed by a lingering ache, a ghost of a love that had abruptly vanished. Daniel.

His name, even silently whispered in her thoughts, was enough to conjure a sharp pang. Their breakup had been a whirlwind of unspoken resentments and simmering frustrations finally boiling over. It wasn't one grand explosion, but a slow, agonizing unraveling. He'd grown distant, preoccupied with his own ambition, the shared dreams they'd once nurtured withering on the vine. Elara felt like a supporting character in his life, her own needs and desires brushed aside. The final confrontation had been a messy, tear-filled affair, filled with accusations and painful truths. Now, adrift in the vastness of the sky, the familiar map of her life had crumbled, leaving her feeling lost and unmoored. This trip, meant to be an escape, now felt like a desperate search for something, anything, to fill the gaping void he had left behind.

Even more so, the memory of Professor Hayes's parting words to her right before graduation still stung. Elara could almost feel the weight of his scrutiny as he'd sat across from her, hands steepled in that characteristic way. He hadn't outright said she lacked talent, but his carefully chosen words had been far more damning. "You have a technical eye, Elara," he'd conceded, "a remarkable understanding of composition and light. But..." He paused, his gaze shifting to some unseen point above her head, "... photography is more than just capturing an image. It's about feeling, about connection. You show me the world, but you don't show me how it *moves* you. I worry, frankly, that you lack the emotional depth required to truly make it in this field let alone pursue your master's in it." His assessment had lingered like a shadowy undercurrent to every success she'd achieved since. Had he been right? Was her work, for all its technical precision, ultimately sterile and devoid of genuine feeling? The question, like a stubborn splinter, continued to prick at the back of her mind.

Her thoughts were interrupted by the captain announcing over the intercom, "We will land in 5 minutes. Local time is 2:30 p.m., mostly sunny, 89 degrees. Thank you for flying with Coral Coast Airways. Enjoy your stay on Isla del Sol." She glanced out the airplane window, seeing blue waters and tiny islands below. As the airplane continued its descent. She took a deep breath, feeling a sense of liberation and anticipation for the journey ahead.

As she stepped off the plane, a wave of elation and relief washed over her. The intense heat greeted her like a warm embrace, instantly hitting her face. She took a deep breath, and the unmistakable scent of salt water lingered in the air, filling her senses with the promise of the ocean nearby. It was a moment of pure joy and anticipation, the beginning of a new adventure.

Elara squinted against the sudden glare as she emerged from the terminal. Pulling her sunglasses from her purse, she moved with purpose towards baggage claim, her mind already picturing the quiet beaches she'd researched. The island's lack of mass appeal surprised her, but it was a welcome sight. She had deliberately sought out Isla del Sol, a place that promised unspoiled natural beauty, far removed from the predictable fanfare of packed hotels and all-inclusive resorts. Here, she knew, the limited number of hotels alongside the abundant villas and cabanas would allow her a genuine experience of island life, not just a curated vacation.

Elara wasn't used to this amount of humidity, but the salty air was a reminder of a promise that the ocean was close by. "What could be better?" she thought to herself as she quickly made her way to baggage claim and then to the car rental place to get her vehicle.

"This is it; this is what she needed," she thought as she got into her rental car and set up the GPS to guide her through the island to her temporary home. All her apprehension quickly dissipated as she meandered along the coastal highway, taking in the blues of the water crashing against the boulders below. It was mesmerizing—she had never seen water so beautiful and clean before. This alone affirmed her decision to travel to a less popular destination, where the natural beauty remained untouched by the construction of hotel after hotel, preserving the essence of the landscape like the sands of time.

"Turn right in 300 meters," her GPS reminded her. " You have reached your final destination," it said as she turned off the car and made her way to the office to check-in.

A cheerful female voice greeted her. "Welcome to Sun Kissed Beach Resorts! My name is Kim and I am the owner of this fine establishment. Checking in?"

Elara took a deep breath, trying to steady the fluttering in her chest. The lobby of the charming guesthouse was warm and welcoming, yet her nerves betrayed the confidence she had felt just moments ago. She clutched the strap of her travel bag, her knuckles whitening as she mentally berated herself for the sudden wave of anxiety. She nodded and stammered, "D-Davis, Elara Davis."

The receptionist, a middle-aged woman with kind eyes and a warm smile, glanced at her computer screen and then back at Elara. "Welcome, Ms. Davis. We're delighted to have you here. It's always exciting to see new faces from far away."

Elara managed a weak smile in return. "Thank you. It's, um, my first time here. First time traveling alone, actually," she admitted, her voice barely above a whisper.

The receptionist's smile widened. "You're in for a wonderful adventure. The first step is always the hardest, but it's worth it. Now, let me get you checked in so you can start exploring."

As Elara watched the receptionist efficiently key in her details, she felt a mixture of trepidation and anticipation. This journey was going to be a true test of her courage and independence. She had no choice but to face it head-on.

As Kim input the final details into the computer system she presented Elara with a set of keys to her villa. "Your villa is named Pink Sands. If you proceed along the cobblestone path, you will encounter a series of colorful villas, with the pink one designated for you. The villa is equipped with all the essentials for your stay. A local market is located ten minutes to the south, where you can fulfill all your grocery requirements. Should you have any questions or encounter any issues, please feel free to call me. I reside upstairs, and you are welcome to reach out at any time, day or night, in case of an emergency."

Elara couldn't help but admire the picturesque surroundings as she approached her villa. The cobblestone path wound through a charming array of vibrantly colored villas, each one unique and inviting. When she reached the pink villa, she was struck by its whimsical charm.

The exterior was a soft pastel pink, with white shutters and a wrap-around porch adorned with hanging flower baskets brimming with colorful blooms. The sound of the ocean waves crashing gently in the distance added to the serene ambiance.

Inside, the villa was cozy and welcoming. The living room featured plush, comfortable furniture in soothing shades of blue and beige, mirroring the seaside theme. Large windows let in plenty of natural light, and from every angle, there was a view of the sparkling ocean. The kitchen was modern and well-equipped, ready for Elara to whip up any meal she desired.

There were touches of local art throughout the villa, giving it a personalized and homey feel. The bedroom was a tranquil haven with a large, inviting bed covered in crisp, white linens and accented with soft pastel throw pillows. A sliding door led to a private patio where Elara could relax and enjoy the ocean breeze.

Elara took a deep breath, savoring the salty sea air and the sense of accomplishment she felt. She had made it to Pink Sands, and a new adventure was just beginning.

Chapter 2: Unexpected Command

For many years, he'd journeyed to Isla del Sol, reveling in each visit. But this time was different. This time, he was headed there not by choice, but by his father's command. "*Son*," his father's voice boomed over the phone. "I've sent all the equipment and supplies you'll need. You, my boy, are going to spend the summer on Isla del Sol, staying with your Aunt Kim, and helping her repair a villa that desperately needs fixing." There had been no asking if he could go, there was just the command, "Pack your bags. Your ticket has been brought and this is when your flight leaves. Take a taxi to your aunt's where a vehicle will be waiting for you to use at your disposal."

Liam had wanted to protest, to argue that his place was at the business, but he knew his father's mantra by heart: "Family first. Family above all else. Family supports family." Even so, he couldn't shake the feeling of being cast aside, like a pawn in a game he didn't fully understand. He wanted to ask his father, "Why me? Why now?" but kept his mouth shut. Instead, Liam decided to ask him, "But what about the company Dad? Who's going to be in charge if I am on the island for an unknown amount of time? I have bids for jobs I am waiting to hear back on."

Liam's father responded firmly, "Liam, I will take charge. This company was mine before I entrusted it to you, and I can readily resume my role, especially since my retirement is still fresh."

The unspoken frustration churned within him. The recent transition of leadership had been anything but smooth. He'd painstakingly tried to earn the crew's respect, to prove he could fill his father's shoes, but the old guard hadn't fully embraced the change, their resistance a constant, low-grade hum in the background. Now, with his father stepping back in, it felt as though his efforts, his sacrifices, were being dismissed.

This trip to Isla del Sol was more than just a summer away. It was a humiliating retreat, a glaring reminder that he still had much to prove and that his father, for all his talk of family, still didn't have complete faith in him.

"Did his father truly think that sending him to Isla del Sol for work was in the company's best interest?" he thought to himself. "What about the changes that he had already implemented? Was his father going to run this ship the way he wanted it run or was he going to revert to the old ways while he was gone?"

The more that Liam sat and pondered everything the angrier he became. This was not how he had imagined his summer going. If anything, Liam had envisioned a summer packed with long, hot hours working on-site with his crew and taking meetings about possible new projects. He wanted to elevate Blue Peak Construction in a way that redefined luxury. He didn't want luxury to only be for the homestead, but for commercial use as well. He wanted the opportunity to build luxury office buildings, but he knew that he might not get that chance now if his dad undid all the months of hard work Liam had put in to move the company forward.

His hands clenched together in anger. There was no way he was going to be able to hide his disappointment but he vowed to make the best of the situation. No, he was going to give his aunt the Blue Peak Construction special, the one that showed people that the company cares and goes above and beyond what was expected of them. His father might've sent him here to help family out, but Liam was instead going to treat this like any other job, his father be damned.

Liam hurried off the plane and headed towards Baggage Claim to collect his luggage and grab a taxi. He wasn't worried about waiting for a taxi to arrive because he knew very well that there were taxis readily available.

After hailing a taxi, Liam told the driver, "Sun Kissed Beach Resorts please." The taxi driver nodded in affirmation, "Yes, sir. First time on the island?"

Liam tried to hide his eye roll behind his sunglasses as he thought, "Why me?" His voice quavered, "No, I have been here many times. This time though is for business, not pleasure." He inhaled as he thought to himself, "Maybe now this guy can leave me alone. I don't have time for idle chit-chat."

No, Liam wasn't in the best of moods, but then again why should he be following the decision his dad made for him without even allowing Liam to have a voice? He was 25 not 5, that should account for something shouldn't it?

By the time he arrived at Sun Kissed Beach Resorts, he was relieved to be out of the taxi since the driver desperately tried to hold a conversation with him since leaving the airport. The driver did not take the hint when Liam wouldn't respond to him that he was not interested in holding a conversation.

As angry as he was about being here thanks to his father, there was something magical about Isla del Sol that resonated with him on a spiritual level. Just standing there in front of the guesthouse he could smell the salty air and caw of the seagulls. Nature was all around him and if he stopped to listen carefully he could hear every magical sound that nature created here. Yes, this place resonated with him every time he visited, and he'd leave a changed man.

Walking into the guesthouse he found his Aunt Kim working away on the computer and noticed her smile as she looked up at him. "Liam!" she exclaimed as she got up and gave him a warm hug. "Thank you for coming. I know your father didn't give you much choice, but *I* told him to ask you not demand it of you."

Liam snorted and thought to himself, "It figures, typical dad." Liam adored his aunt and always wondered how she could be his father's sister since they were opposite personalities. Kim had always been the "cool aunt" who provided Liam with the outlet to be himself away from her brother's strict rules. She was more carefree and didn't conform to societal norms. No, Kim was the type of person who loved adventure, but just like her brother, valued family.

His dad on the other hand believed in rigorous structure and routine, something that he expected from others, especially Liam. No, his dad was all about authority, and always seemed to have a serious expression on his face. Liam couldn't recall the last time he had seen his father smile or even congratulate him on a job well done. His dad was extremely pragmatic whereas his Aunt Kim was more visionary. His dad believed in strict order and Kim was just the opposite, she tended to go with the flow of things and let them happen as they should.

Kim's decision to live abroad was driven by her desire to escape societal expectations, especially those imposed by her older brother, Pete. Unlike Pete, she believed in allowing people to be themselves. Every time Liam visited, Kim treated him with kindness, understanding the pressure he faced from Pete. She had warned Pete multiple times that his rigid expectations would only push Liam away, but her words fell on deaf ears. Now, with Liam here, it was evident that his presence was not by choice but a result of Pete's insistence, rather than a genuine invitation as Kim had suggested.

Liam embraced his Aunt Kim warmly. "Hi, Aunt Kim. Thanks for having me."

"Oh, Liam," Aunt Kim replied, returning the hug with a smile. "You're family and always welcome here. I just wish your father had given you the choice instead of demanding you come."

"Aunt Kim, please," Liam said, his voice filled with affection. "I would've come regardless. It's for you."

She smiled warmly at him. "I know. I just feel bad for taking you away from the company right after Pete put you in charge."

Liam shook his head and smiled, "Don't worry about it. I'm here now and you are going to get the full Blue Peak Construction treatment."

His aunt laughed out loud. "You sound just like your father now in the best way possible Liam. Here are the keys to the truck for you to use while here. You are more than welcome to crash upstairs with me or stay in the villa that you are going to be working on. Your choice."

Liam laughed boisterously. "Can I still come over for meals? I mean, you make some of the best food around."

Kim just shook her head and laughed as she tossed him the keys to the truck and then grabbed the keys for Azure Cove and tossed them to him as well. "All the supplies are in the villa waiting for you. You know you are more than welcome to come over anytime you want for food."

Liam hugged his aunt and kissed her on the cheek. "Maybe this wasn't going to be unbearable after all," he thought as he got in the truck and drove down the cobblestone path toward Azure Cove.

Liam had spent many summers here at Sun Kissed Beach Resorts and each villa had its unique personality. He was curious to see what work needed to be done to Azure Cove since he couldn't recall it needing fixing a couple of years ago.

The first thing that Liam noticed was that his aunt had repainted the villa next door. Pink Sands no longer was this bright tropical pink but a more subdued pastel pink that mimicked the color of the sand and he smiled, he loved the new color of Pink Sands and wondered what other changes she had made. Upon closer inspection, Liam noticed he was going to have to do some repairs to the wrap-around deck on Azure Cove. He wondered after seeing the new paint job to Pink Sands if Azure Cove should be repainted a different blue, something more muted but reflective of the waters instead of this bright turquoise color on it now.

Inside the villa, he looked around and noticed that his aunt had removed all the wall decorations, and rightfully so, since this place needed a refresh. The tiles on the floor were cracked and he was going to have to replace them, and hopefully be able to match the existing tile, unless his father had already sent new tile. The bathroom was in working condition but could also use a refresh. The more he looked around the more he made a mental running list of things to fix or improve upon.

Liam didn't need much to feel comfortable—just a working shower, a toilet, and a bed to sleep in. He planned on working long hours and hoped the neighboring guests wouldn't be too annoyed with him. Smiling to himself, he felt a surge of satisfaction as ideas began to take shape. He had no clue what the overall plan was or what his father had shipped from the States, but he was ready to dive in. "No time like the present," he said aloud to no one in particular as he started opening the containers his father had sent.

As Liam unpacked the containers, he began to understand what he needed to focus on. His smile widened when he discovered his father's notebook—the one he used for jotting down information for bids. With the notebook in hand, Liam took a moment to create various to-do lists, detailing what he had to accomplish versus what he'd like to do with the villa. He knew the task ahead would be painstaking but necessary. Having a running list would keep him on track.

Chapter 3: Island Discoveries

With a deep breath, Elara began unpacking her essentials. She carefully placed her clothes in the wardrobe and arranged her toiletries in the bathroom, finding a sense of satisfaction in the simple task. It was hard to comprehend that something as mundane as putting her clothes and toiletries away could give her as much joy as it had.

With her essentials unpacked, Elara felt a surge of excitement about exploring the island. Grabbing her tote bag and keys, she decided to head out to the local market for supplies. As she drove along the winding coastal road, the vibrant landscape unfolded around her. To her right, the azure ocean stretched out to meet the horizon, the waves sparkling under the sun's golden rays. Pink sand beaches lined with palm trees swayed gently in the breeze, inviting her to relax and unwind.

On her left, lush green mountains rose majestically, covered in dense foliage and vibrant tropical flowers in every color imaginable. The scent of hibiscus and frangipani filled the air, mingling with the salty tang of the sea. Elara passed through small villages where colorful houses stood in neat rows, their cheerful facades a testament to the island's lively culture.

Friendly locals waved as she drove by, their smiles as bright as the sun overhead. This unexpected warmth was a pleasant surprise. Soon, she arrived at a bustling market where vendors showcased an array of fresh fruits and vegetables. The air was filled with laughter, lively conversation, and the occasional strumming of a guitar. Elara moved from stall to stall, selecting fresh produce and a few local delicacies to try.

Elara's excitement surged the moment she stepped into the bustling market. The explosion of vibrant colors, tantalizing aromas, and lively chatter enveloped her in a sensory feast unlike anything she had ever encountered. She regretted not bringing her camera to immortalize the myriad of sights and sounds, each teeming with life and story. The market was a vivid mosaic of cultures, with stalls overflowing with exotic spices, handmade crafts, and delectable treats. As she wandered through the animated scene, Professor Hayes' criticism resonated with her—her previous work lacked the richness and depth that only firsthand experiences could infuse. This connection transforms a photograph into an emotion. Elara longed to capture the essence of this enchanting place, to freeze the fleeting moments, and preserve the kaleidoscope of emotions she experienced in that instant.

She knew that the market was a place she'd return to time and again during her stay on Isla del Sol. The bustling open-air market, with its lively street vendors and vibrant colors, was a captivating mosaic of meticulously handcrafted tapestries. Each tapestry told a story, a testament to the island's rich history and culture, passed down through generations. She longed to talk to the artisans, to learn how they wove their intricate patterns and made their delicious delicacies. She wanted to capture these moments with her camera, creating memories that would remind her, in her later years, of the profound impact this culture and history had on her.

Returning to the villa with her provisions, Elara felt a deep sense of accomplishment. As she unpacked her groceries and neatly arranged them in the kitchen, she knew she was ready to settle in and make this place her own. The charm of the villa enveloped her, and she couldn't shake the feeling that this adventure was just beginning. Memories of the market's vibrant energy continued to dance in her mind, and she realized that the experience had already started to transform her. The world now seemed bigger, richer, and more intricate than she had ever imagined. Elara understood that this journey was more than just a physical one; it was an exploration of her senses, perspectives, and aspirations. With a newfound sense of purpose and excitement, she embraced the promise of what lay ahead, eager to see how this adventure would shape her future.

As Elara ventured to the bustling market from her villa, Liam remained in the neighboring villa, diligently crafting notes about the renovations it needed. They had not yet met, but both enjoyed magnificent views of the ocean—a serene backdrop to their bustling lives.

Liam, raised in the business by his father, absorbed invaluable lessons over the years. Now, seated at the table which acted as his desk, he was determined to turn the villa into a masterpiece. This project was his alone—a testament to his ambition and skill.

Recalling his father's teachings on craftsmanship and resilience, Liam felt a surge of determination. His drive for perfection mirrored his father's, an unspoken tribute to the man who had shaped him. This project was his chance to prove that he had inherited his father's tenacity and skill.

The villa, once a haven of relaxation, had now become the command center for his restoration efforts. Each page of his notebook reflected meticulous planning and an unwavering commitment to his goals. As the sun cast long shadows across the room, Liam felt the weight of responsibility more acutely. Every decision mattered, and the stakes were high.

Just as his father once approached his projects with fervor and dedication, Liam did the same. The villa's transformation was not merely a renovation; it was a manifestation of his vision and hard work. He saw each challenge as an opportunity to prove to himself and his father that he had what it took to excel in their shared passion.

Elara, gathering supplies at the market, was unaware of the connection their paths would soon share. For Liam, the restoration of the villa was more than just a project—it was a tribute to his father and a testament to the depth of his abilities. With every painstaking effort, he was ready to transform the villa into a stunning sanctuary

Later that afternoon, Elara returned and settled on a sun lounger outside her villa, basking in the warmth and tranquility of the ocean view. Liam noticed her from his window, her serene presence contrasting with the bustling market scene earlier. He felt a curious pull but hesitated to say anything just yet. For now, he simply admired her from a distance, wondering what paths might unfold in the days to come.

As the day drew to a close, Liam stepped outside to watch the sunset. The sky was a canvas of vibrant hues, reflected beautifully on the water's surface. To his surprise, he saw Elara with her camera, capturing the breathtaking scene. He paused, captivated by both the beauty of the sunset and the sight of Elara immersed in her photography. A smile tugged at his lips as he watched her, locked in her photographer's gaze, appreciating the moment without disturbing the tranquility.

Elara didn't notice Liam standing there, admiring both her and the sunset. He was mesmerized by her beauty and the way she focused intently through her camera lens. At that moment, he couldn't help but feel that fate was gently weaving their lives together, bringing these two lost souls closer with each passing day.

Liam had come to Isla del Sol under duress, a trip imposed by his father. But now, here was this captivating woman who had captured his attention. Maybe, just maybe, this trip wouldn't be so bad after all, he thought to himself. He wanted to know more about her. Why was she here alone? What stories did she carry? He wondered if he should ask his aunt what she could tell him about the intriguing woman next door in the Pink Sands villa.

Since Liam was already taking a break, he decided to hop in the truck and drive up to his aunt's apartment for some food, and maybe see what she could tell him about the beauty staying in the villa next to him. The island's warm breeze rustled through the palm trees as he drove, the golden hues of sunset painting the sky. He was intrigued by Elara and wanted the chance to meet her if it was at all possible. All he needed was a little bit of information from his aunt. He knew this trip was for business, not pleasure, but why couldn't he take some time occasionally to meet a beautiful woman?

Chapter 4: Unseen Connections

Liam parked his truck outside his aunt's charming apartment, the scent of her famous empanadas wafting through the open windows. As he walked in, he found her bustling around the kitchen, a warm smile spreading across her face.
"Liam, my dear! I was wondering when you'd show up," she said, wiping her hands on a towel and pulling him into a hug.
"Aunt Kim, it's always good to see you," Liam replied, returning the hug. "And you know I can't resist your cooking."
Kim chuckled and gestured for him to sit at the kitchen table. "Sit, sit! I'll get you a plate."
As they settled into a comfortable rhythm, Liam decided it was time to bring up the topic on his mind. "Aunt Kim, can I ask you something?"
"Of course, anything," she said, her eyes twinkling with curiosity.
"There's this woman staying in the Pink Sands villa next to mine," Liam began, trying to keep his tone casual. "I noticed her a few times today and... well, I was wondering if you knew anything about her."
Kim paused, a knowing smile playing on her lips. "Ah, the mysterious beauty with the camera. Her name is Elara, and she just arrived today like you. She booked her stay last minute for an entire month. She seemed a bit nervous when she checked in, almost like she was trying to run from her ghosts if you catch my drift."
Liam nodded, something he could appreciate. He was here on business and if he got to meet Elara, then it would happen. "So, about the project," he began, switching gears. "Am I supposed to pick out the paint colors, or do you have them already?"
Kim thought for a moment. "I can pick the colors out unless you have some suggestions," she said.

Liam thought for a moment. "Hm, well how do you feel about repainting the exterior of the villa? Are you for or against it?"

Kim's frustration broke through. "Liam, didn't your father mention anything about this?" She took a breath and offered a quick apology. "I'm sorry, Liam...your father had a list of tasks from me, and painting the whole villa, inside and out, was on it."

With a gentle smile, he placed his hand on top of Aunt Kim's, "Aunt Kim," he reassured softly, "It's alright. Let's finish our dinner first, then we can head outside to enjoy the evening. We can discuss your wishes and my suggestions. Does that sound good?"

She smiled at him, "You're a good nephew Liam. Thank you."

Once dinner was finished, Liam and his aunt settled outside, savoring the warm tropical breeze of the evening. As he breathed deeply, Liam could distinguish the alluring scents of plumeria and the intense fragrance of nightshade jasmine. These aromas, carried on the far-reaching breezes, wove through the island, creating an enchanting tapestry of fragrance. The intoxicating scents reminded Liam that Isla del Sol was his home away from home, a canvas brimming with opportunity.

"Aunt Kim, let's start off easy, shall we?" Liam asked about painting the exterior of the villa. "Did you want to keep the same shade of blue, or are you thinking of a different one?"

She smiled. "Oh, that's easy. I want a blue that's more muted, similar to what I did with Pink Sands."

Liam nodded. "Alright, perfect. I'll show you a few different color ideas in the morning. How about the door? Do you want to make a statement with it?"

She paused to consider. "When you show me the house colors, pick two options for the door: one that makes a dramatic statement and one that's more subtle."

Liam smiled, happy to see that he and his aunt were off to a good start. "Now, the wrap-around deck I see I need to just do some repairs, do you want it to be painted, or stained? Both options you need to maintain, the only difference is one won't need to be done yearly."

"Oh, that's easy, stain. You can pick the stain. I trust you, Liam."

Liam nodded, appreciating the praise his aunt had already given him. "So, moving inside to the kitchen. Are we getting new cabinets, or are we refinishing the current ones and adding a new countertop, sink, and hardware?"

"Um," she began, then paused. "The cabinets are in good shape and just need a refresh, but we'll have to replace the stove. So, why don't we do this: I'll look for a stove and give you the measurements, then you can tell me if we need to adjust the cabinets to fit it. This might change our approach to the kitchen. Unless, of course, you'd like to join me in looking at stoves?"

Liam laughed. "You're not used to being this involved, are you?"

Kim shook her head no and chuckled. "No, your father was tell me the bare minimum and then let me do my thing."

Liam huffed. "And that, Aunt Kim, is one difference between me and my father. I want my clients to be hands-on and give me their input. It helps me create a more cohesive design."

"And you will be excellent running the company when you get back. I do not doubt that."

Liam beamed, greatly appreciative of his aunt. "Now, let's talk about the cracked tiles on the floor. Do you have any extras, or should we consider laying down an entirely new floor?"

"Oh, that's simple," his aunt said with a proud smile. "I have extras. I made sure to stock up with extra tiles just in case."

Liam chuckled at his aunt's reaction. "Got it, we'll use the extras then. That should make things easier. Anything else? New lights? New fans? Anything?"

His aunt shook her head no. "That was easy."

Liam smiled suddenly glad to be here on Isla del Sol working on this project. Overall, it didn't seem too bad. Yes, he was going to have to put in some long days sometimes, but maybe he would be able to even find the time to meet the beautiful Elara. Already he was feeling much better about this forced visit to Isla del Sol.

While Liam was visiting his aunt, Elara seized the moment to prepare a simple yet satisfying dinner for herself. She decided to dine outside, wanting to immerse herself in the island's enchanting atmosphere. As she gazed up at the night sky, thousands of stars sparkled like diamonds, creating a breathtaking tapestry above. The air was filled with the sweet fragrance of plumeria and night jasmine, the same scents that Liam was inhaling not far away. This moment, under the twinkling heavens of Isla del Sol, was one she knew she would treasure forever. Back home, the night sky never shone with such mesmerizing brilliance, nor did it carry the same intoxicating aromas.

While Liam was visiting his aunt, Elara seized the moment to prepare a simple yet satisfying dinner for herself. She decided to dine outside, wanting to immerse herself in the island's enchanting atmosphere. As she gazed up at the night sky, thousands of stars sparkled like diamonds, creating a breathtaking tapestry above. The air was filled with the sweet fragrance of plumeria and night jasmine, the same scents that Liam was inhaling not far away. This moment, under the twinkling heavens of Isla del Sol, was one she knew she would treasure forever. Back home, the night sky never shone with such mesmerizing brilliance, nor did it carry the same intoxicating aromas.

As she looked at the stars, her thoughts wandered to everything that had happened recently. The breakup with Daniel still stung, but here, under this vast and peaceful sky, the pain felt a little more distant. She also recalled the harsh criticism from Professor Hayes, words that had once cut deep. Yet now, in this moment of tranquility, those criticisms seemed so inconsequential. Here, surrounded by the beauty of Isla del Sol, she found a sense of solace that she hadn't felt in a long time.

She sighed out loud. There wasn't anybody around to hear her, but that was fine. For the first time in years, she was alone. There was no Daniel, just Elara. But that was alright; she somehow knew that fate had given her this opportunity here in Isla del Sol to learn about what was truly important to her and her life.

If she only knew that the same fate was already at work weaving its spell on Liam as it was with her. Both had yet to meet, but fate would soon weave that chance meeting.

Chapter 5: Settling In

Liam awoke to the soft glow of the early morning sun streaming through his window. Stretching, he felt a sense of purpose and excitement about the day ahead. Today, he would head to his aunt's to show her paint samples for the villa and shop for a new stove—tasks that would mark the beginning of his renovation project on Isla del Sol. While eating breakfast, Liam spotted Elara outside in her robe, sipping a cup of coffee. With a smile at the familiar sight, he wondered what it would be like to meet the raven-haired beauty for the first time. Finishing his meal, he grabbed his keys and headed out. The morning air was fresh and invigorating as he rolled the windows down in the truck, allowing the scent of saltwater and tropical flowers to fill his senses.

Meanwhile, at the Pink Sands villa, Elara was easing into her morning routine. She stood outside on the patio, wrapped in a plush robe, savoring the warmth of her coffee mug in her hands. The sun was just beginning to rise, casting a golden hue over the island and illuminating the lush landscape. The tranquil morning air was filled with the sweet fragrance of plumeria and night jasmine, remnants of the previous night. Elara took a deep breath, feeling a sense of peace and clarity that had eluded her for so long. She reflected on the events that had led her here, her thoughts drifting to her recent breakup with Daniel and the harsh criticism from Professor Hayes. Yet, under the serene sky of Isla del Sol, those past troubles seemed to fade away.

Unbeknownst to her, Liam had spotted her from his vantage point while he had breakfast at the villa's outdoor dining area. He was captivated by her serene presence, wrapped in her robe, appearing almost ethereal in the soft morning light. Had Elara known she was being watched; she would have been mortified at the thought of someone seeing her in such a private moment.

Arriving at his aunt's apartment, Liam found her already bustling around, clearing her breakfast so that they had room to spread out the various paint samples.

"Liam, good morning!" Aunt Kim greeted him with a cheerful smile. "Ready to get started?"

"Absolutely," Liam replied, his enthusiasm clear. "Let's see what we've got for the villa."

Together, they pored over the paint samples, discussing hues and finishes. Kim shared her thoughts on the muted blue she envisioned for the exterior, and Liam presented a few options for the front door, both dramatic and subtle.

"By the way, Aunt Kim," Liam asked, glancing up from the samples, "do you have clients checking in and out today, or are you free to look at stoves with me?"

Once they made their selections, they headed out to the local hardware store to finalize their choices and pick up a new stove. As they drove, they chatted about the renovation plans, the island's charm, and the possibilities for the villa. Liam felt a deep sense of contentment—working alongside his aunt, breathing in the island's essence, and contributing to its beauty.

After finishing her morning coffee and enjoying the peaceful sunrise, Elara felt a renewed sense of adventure. She decided that today would be perfect for exploring the island and soaking in the sun on the famous pink sands of Isla del Sol.

Elara packed a small backpack with essentials: her camera, a journal, a bottle of water, and a light snack. She slipped into a comfortable sundress and sandals, ready to embrace the day's possibilities. As she stepped outside, the warm tropical sun kissed her skin, and the gentle breeze carried the sweet fragrance of hibiscus and frangipani.

Her first stop was a quaint local market she had spotted on her arrival. The vibrant stalls were filled with colorful fruits, handmade crafts, and friendly islanders eager to share their stories. Elara wandered through the market, capturing the lively scenes with her camera and chatting with the vendors. She picked up a few souvenirs, including a handcrafted bracelet that caught her eye.

With the sun climbing higher in the sky, Elara made her way to the island's famous pink sand beach. The sight of the soft, blush-colored sand meeting the crystal-clear waters was breathtaking. She found a secluded spot, laid out her towel, and settled in for a day of relaxation. The rhythmic sound of the waves was soothing, and Elara felt a deep sense of peace as she basked in the sun's warmth.

After a while, she took a leisurely swim in the calm waters, feeling the refreshing embrace of the ocean. She floated on her back, feeling the sun kiss her skin as she gazed up at the clear blue sky. Her mind wandered to the possibilities that lay ahead. The island felt like a sanctuary, a place where she could heal and rediscover herself.

In the afternoon, Elara decided to explore more of the island. She hiked along a scenic trail that led to a stunning viewpoint overlooking the coastline. The sun was warm on her skin as she reached the top. From this vantage point, she could see the full beauty of Isla del Sol—a perfect blend of lush greenery, pink sands, and turquoise waters. She saw sailboats dotting the horizon, their sails a stark contrast to the blue of the sky. The sound of birds filled the air, and she watched a bird dive into the water and come up with a fish in its beak. She couldn't wait to explore the jungle at some point.

Elara noticed a dilapidated, weathered lighthouse on the edge of the cliff. It screamed of history. She wondered if it had once warned other ships of the rocks at night or served as a beacon for the pirates of old. It was a spot she knew she would have to explore. She took a moment to capture the scene with her camera, knowing these photos would serve as cherished memories.

As the day drew to a close, Elara made her way back to the villa, feeling a sense of fulfillment and contentment. She had embraced the island's beauty and tranquility, and she knew that this was just the beginning of her journey.

As she approached the Pink Sands villa, she noticed the sound of construction work coming from the villa next door. Curious, she paused for a moment, listening to the distant hum of machinery and the occasional hammer strike. To her surprise, she found the rhythmic noises surprisingly soothing, a unique backdrop to the tranquil island life. It seemed that renovations were underway, and she wondered who was behind the project.

She was even more intrigued when she noticed there was only one truck at the villa, the same truck she recognized from yesterday. Little did she know that fate was already at work, weaving its magic on both her and Liam. Their paths had yet to cross, but the island's enchanting charm would soon bring them together.

The rhythmic sound of the waves crashing against the shore mingled with the construction noises, creating a unique symphony of island life. The scent of fresh paint and sawdust wafted through the air, mixing with the salty breeze. She couldn't help but feel a sense of anticipation, knowing that something significant was about to happen.

Suddenly, the sky darkened as a tropical rain shower swept over the island. The heavy droplets pelted down, creating a symphony of splashes against the leaves and the villa's roof. Elara hurried inside, watching as the downpour transformed the landscape, washing away any traces of the morning's tranquility. Yet, as quickly as it began, the rain ceased, giving way to the bright afternoon sun once again. The air was thick with humidity, and a vibrant rainbow arched across the sky, adding a touch of magic to the moment. Elara grabbed her camera, eager to capture the rainbow against the backdrop of the tropical oasis. She stepped back outside, feeling the warmth of the sun and the wetness of the ground beneath her feet, marveling at how the island's weather could change so swiftly and beautifully.

She was mesmerized, even transformed, by this weather. It was a phenomenon she was not used to—sudden tropical showers that gave way to beautiful skies and rainbows. It was a stark contrast to the familiar suburban college life she had known. She just wanted to go outside and giggle like a little girl, the feeling now not lost on her.

As the skies rapidly opened up, Liam took a moment to ensure no tools were left outside to be ruined by the rain. Despite his many visits to Isla del Sol, he was still amazed by how swiftly a rainstorm could roll in and then dissipate, leaving behind a renewed sense of nature. This was island life, as it had been for centuries and as it would continue to be long after he was gone. The island's timeless rhythm of sudden storms and serene beauty was a testament to its enduring spirit, a cycle that remained unchanged by the passage of time and the fleeting presence of visitors like Liam.

Chapter 6: Converging Paths

One Week Later

Liam wiped the sweat from his brow as he stepped back to admire the progress on the villa. What was once a dilapidated structure was slowly transforming into a charming retreat. Each day presented new challenges, but the sense of accomplishment made every moment of hard work worth it. The exterior paint had dried to a perfect muted blue, accentuated by the vibrant color of the front door.

Inside, the kitchen had undergone a remarkable transformation. Liam had meticulously sanded and stained the cabinets to reveal their natural beauty. He replaced the countertops with sturdy soapstone, an investment he knew would withstand the wear and tear from future renters. The new stove now served as a stunning centerpiece in the freshly renovated kitchen.

Liam's days were filled with the sounds of construction—the rhythmic hammering, the whir of power tools, and the occasional friendly banter with Aunt Kim whenever she would stop by to bring him something to eat or to check on how things were progressing. The villa was becoming a labor of love, and Liam could feel the island's magic infusing every corner of the property.

As he worked, Liam couldn't help but reflect on the whirlwind of events that had brought him to Isla del Sol. The family business had always been a part of his life, a legacy handed down through generations. He remembered the pride in his father's eyes when he first started working alongside him. But that pride had turned into unexpected disappointment when his father suddenly reclaimed the reins of the business, forcing Liam to take on this renovation project as a way to "prove" himself.

Though the task had initially felt like a punishment, the island had begun to work its magic on Liam. The sunsets over the ocean, the gentle lapping of the waves, and the vibrant community of Isla del Sol had given him a sense of peace and purpose he hadn't felt in years. Each stroke of the paintbrush, each piece of wood carefully placed, was imbued with his determination to make something truly beautiful out of a situation that had once seemed bleak.

His father's motto echoed in the back of his mind: **"Family first. Family above all else. Family supports family."** These words, once a source of comfort, now felt like a challenge. Yet, they propelled him forward, reminding him of the legacy he was upholding and the future he was building—not just for himself, but for the generations to come.

Isla del Sol had always been a special place to Liam. It was a place of cherished memories, where family vacations were once filled with laughter and joy. Now, working on the villa alone, he found solace in the familiar sights and sounds of the island. The renovation had become more than just a job; it was a way to reconnect with the past, honor his family's legacy, and carve out a space where future memories could be made.

From his window, Liam occasionally spotted Elara wandering outside her villa. Sometimes she was sunbathing, basking in the warmth of the island's golden rays. Other times, she was photographing the lush nature around her, capturing the island's beauty through her lens. He couldn't help but be intrigued by her presence, wondering what stories and passions she carried with her.

Liam felt a growing curiosity about Elara, a desire to get to know the woman who seemed to find such joy and inspiration in the island's beauty. Yet, he was hesitant. His own insecurities and the weight of his family's expectations held him back. He feared that approaching her might disturb the delicate balance he was trying to build within himself. Still, each time he saw her, a part of him hoped for a chance encounter that might bridge the gap between their solitary journeys.

Meanwhile, Elara had spent the past week immersing herself in the beauty and culture of Isla del Sol. Each morning, she woke up with a sense of adventure, eager to discover what new wonders the island had in store. Her camera became her constant companion, capturing the vibrant life and breathtaking landscapes that surrounded her. Yet still, she felt like there was something out there, something more for her to discover, but what, she didn't quite know.

Today, Elara decided to visit the island's botanical gardens, a hidden gem she had heard about from a local vendor at the market. The gardens were a lush paradise, teeming with exotic plants and vibrant blooms. As she meandered along the winding paths, she marveled at the diversity of flora. Each plant was more stunning than the last, providing a picturesque backdrop for her camera lens.

She paused by a small pond, its surface dotted with delicate water lilies. The tranquil setting provided the perfect backdrop for her photography, and she spent hours capturing the intricate details of the flowers and the play of light on the water. Each click of her camera brought a renewed sense of joy, a reminder of why she had fallen in love with photography in the first place.

Elara's thoughts drifted to Professor Hayes, whose harsh critiques had once shaken her confidence. His words had echoed in her mind for too long, casting shadows over her passion. But here, surrounded by the vibrant beauty of the island, those words began to fade into the background. She felt a growing sense of self-assurance, a quiet confidence that her photographs captured something meaningful and unique.

As the sun began to set, casting a golden glow over the gardens, Elara felt a deep sense of peace. The island had a way of soothing her soul, and she knew that her time here was helping her heal and rediscover her passions. She reviewed the day's photographs, smiling at the moments she had captured. Each image was a testament to her journey—an exploration not just of the island, but of her own resilience and creativity.

The pain of her breakup with Daniel had begun to hurt less, and Elara could now see it for what it was—a catalyst for growth. The relationship had taught her valuable lessons about herself, her desires, and her boundaries. She could now understand the drive and passion that Daniel had, yet she realized that he could never truly understand hers. As she embraced the island's tranquility, she felt herself transforming, growing stronger and more confident as both a person and a woman. The rhythmic clicking of her camera had become a melody of self-discovery, and with each photograph, Elara's confidence grew stronger. She was beginning to trust in her own vision again, to see the world through her lens, unclouded by doubt.

Liam wiped the sweat from his brow as he stepped back to admire the progress on the villa. The renovation was coming along nicely, and he was proud of the work he had put in. As he gathered his tools and prepared to call it a day, he noticed Elara stepping out of her villa next door, her camera slung over her shoulder.

The evening light was perfect, casting a warm glow over the island. Elara seemed to hesitate for a moment, glancing around before her eyes met Liam's. She offered a shy wave, and Liam, feeling a sudden surge of courage, waved back.

"Hi there!" Liam called out, closing the distance between them with a friendly smile. "I'm Liam. I couldn't help but notice you taking photos around the island. You have an eye for beauty."

Elara blushed, her timidity evident as she replied, "Hi, I'm Elara, but my friends call me Ellie. Thank you. I love capturing the essence of places I visit, and Isla del Sol is just so inspiring."

Liam nodded, genuinely intrigued. "I've seen you around with your camera. It looks like you find a lot of joy in what you do."

"Absolutely," Elara said, her voice gaining a bit more confidence. "Photography is my passion. There's something magical about preserving moments in time."

As they chatted, a light breeze rustled the leaves around them, and the scent of blooming flowers filled the air. The conversation flowed naturally, and they discovered shared interests and mutual admiration for the island's beauty. The comfortable silence that occasionally settled between their words felt as natural as if they had known each other for years.

Feeling a surge of inspiration, Liam said, "If you're interested, I'd love to show you the work I've been doing on the villa. It's been quite a project, but it's coming together."

Elara's eyes lit up with curiosity. "I'd love that. It sounds fascinating."

Liam led her to the villa, opening the door to reveal the beautifully renovated space. "This is the kitchen," he said, gesturing to the stained cabinets and soapstone countertops. "I've put a lot of work into making it functional and beautiful."

Elara admired the craftsmanship, her camera in hand. "It's incredible, Liam. You've done an amazing job."

As the days went by, Elara often found herself visiting Liam while he worked, her camera always poised to capture the moments of his dedication and hard work. She would take vivid shots of him sanding wood, painting walls, and carefully installing fixtures. Each photograph told a story of Liam's commitment to the villa—his labor of love.

After each session, Elara and Liam would review the photos together, her ability to capture the rawness of his work constantly amazing him. Liam couldn't help but feel flattered and inspired by Elara's presence. Her eye for detail and knack for capturing the essence of his efforts through her lens made the work feel even more meaningful. As they pored over the images, Liam realized that Elara's photographs could help build his company, showcasing the quality and passion behind his work to potential clients. It was something his father had never once considered, and Liam felt a newfound sense of purpose.

Their bond grew stronger with each shared moment, and the island's magic seemed to weave their lives together in ways they could never have imagined.

Elara couldn't help but notice the long hours that Liam spent working on the villa, or how Kim, the owner of the property would stop by and bring him food to eat. Seeing Kim's visits made Elara wonder if Liam was taking the time to eat and keep his strength up. Normally she was not this forward, but after spending some time with him, she couldn't help but feel as if she had been destined to meet him.

As the sun dipped below the horizon, casting a golden glow across Isla del Sol, Elara found herself standing at the edge of her villa's veranda, gazing out at the ocean. The air was warm, filled with the scent of blooming flowers and the distant sound of waves gently lapping against the shore. She turned her camera in her hands, lost in thought about how much the island and even Liam had come to mean to her.

Tonight, she wanted to do something special, something that would reflect the growing bond she felt with Liam. She had spent the afternoon preparing a meal-an assortment of local dishes she had learned from the island's residents. With everything set up, she took a deep breath and made her way next door.

Liam was just wrapping up his day's work on the villa, wiping his hands clean and admiring the progress he had made. When he saw Elara approaching, he smiled warmly. "Hey, Ellie. How's your day been?"

"Hey Liam," she replied her voice carrying a hint of excitement. "It's been great, thanks. I wanted to ask you something."

Liam raised an eyebrow, intrigued, "What's that?"

Elara took a small step forward, feeling a mix of nerves and anticipation. "I was wondering if you'd like to join me for dinner tonight. I've prepared a meal, and I'd love to share it with you. We can relax, enjoy some good food, and maybe even talk about your amazing renovation work."

A genuine smile spread across Liam's face. "I'd love that, Ellie. It sounds perfect."

"Great! Give me a few minutes to finish setting up, and then come on over," Elara said, her eyes bright with happiness.

Liam nodded, feeling a flutter of excitement. "I'll be there."

A short while later, Liam made his way to Elara's villa. The soft glow of candlelight welcomed him as he stepped inside. The table was beautifully set with a variety of dishes, each one showcasing Elara's effort and thoughtfulness.

"This looks amazing," Liam said, genuinely impressed.

"Thank you," Elara replied, a touch of blush on her cheeks. "I hope you enjoy it."

As they sat down to eat, the conversation flowed easily. They shared stories, laughed, and found themselves opening up to each other in ways they hadn't before. The evening was filled with moments of connection and understanding, and by the time the meal was over, both Elara and Liam felt a deep sense of contentment.

As the night deepened, the soft glow of the candles cast dancing shadows on the walls. Elara and Liam found themselves leaning a little closer, their conversations becoming more intimate.

Elara's heart fluttered each time Liam's gaze lingered on her. She felt a warmth spreading through her, but with it came a twinge of uncertainty. She glanced down at her hands, nervously twisting a napkin between her fingers. "You know, it's been a while since I've felt this comfortable around someone new."

Liam nodded his heart racing. "I know what you mean. Being here, talking to you, it feels...different. In a good way."

There was a pause, filled with the gentle hum of the night. Elara's eyes flickered to Liam's, finding a mixture of warmth and hesitation in his gaze. She wanted to reach out, to bridge the distance between them, but she was afraid of disrupting the delicate balance they had found.

Liam cleared his throat, a nervous laugh escaping him. "I guess I'm just...cautious. It's been a long time since I've let myself get close to someone."

Elara's smile was understanding, yet her eyes revealed a hint of her vulnerability. "Me too. It's scary, isn't it? Letting someone in after being hurt."

Liam's hand moved slightly as if he wanted to reach out and hold hers, but he stopped himself. "Yeah, it is. But maybe...maybe it's worth the risk."

Elara felt her heart skip a beat at his words. She took a deep breath, trying to steady her nerves. "I think so too."

Liam stood up, offering his hand to Elara. "How about a walk on the beach? It's a beautiful night."

Elara smiled, taking his hand as she stood. "I'd love that."

They walked side by side along the beach behind the villas, the sand cool beneath their feet and the sound of the waves creating a soothing backdrop. The moonlight cast a silvery glow on the water, and the stars above seemed to twinkle just for them.

As they strolled, their conversation flowed naturally, touching on their dreams, fears, and the unexpected paths that had led them to Isla del Sol. The more they talked, the more they realized how much they had in common and how much they enjoyed each other's company.

After a while, they stopped, standing close together as they gazed out at the ocean. The moment felt perfect, suspended in time. Liam turned to Elara, his eyes searching hers for a sign.

Elara felt her heart race, but she didn't look away. Instead, she took a small step closer. "Liam, there's something I want to share with you."

Liam looked at her, his expression open and understanding. "What is it, Ellie?"

She took a deep breath, gathering her thoughts. "I went through a tough breakup not too long ago. Daniel and I were together for a while, and I thought he understood, my passion for photography. But it turns out, he couldn't quite grasp it. It left me questioning myself and my dreams."

Liam listened intently, his heart aching for her. "I'm sorry you went through that, Ellie. It's never easy to have someone you care about not understand you."

Elara nodded, her eyes reflecting the moonlight. "It was hard, but coming here, to Isla del Sol, has been healing. And meeting you... it's been unexpectedly wonderful."

Liam smiled softly. "I'm glad you're here, Ellie. And for what it's worth, I see your passion. It's inspiring."

Feeling a newfound connection, Elara took another step closer. "Liam, what about you? You mentioned your father before."

Liam sighed, his expression growing thoughtful. "Yeah, my dad and I... we have a complicated relationship. The family business was everything to him, and I always wanted to prove myself to him. But when he took back control, it felt like a punch to the gut. Coming here to work on the villa was supposed to be a punishment, but it's become so much more."

Elara squeezed his hand gently. "It's amazing what you've done here. You're building something beautiful, not just for your family, but for yourself."

Liam's eyes softened. "Thank you, Ellie. That means a lot."

Elara took a deep breath, deciding to open up further. "I had a professor, Professor Hayes, who was incredibly harsh with his critiques. He made me doubt myself and my photography. But being here, capturing the beauty of Isla del Sol, has helped me rediscover my confidence."

Liam looked at her with admiration. "You're an incredible photographer, Ellie. Don't let anyone make you doubt that."

Feeling a deep sense of connection, Elara took another step closer, her breath catching as Liam gently cupped her cheek. The world seemed to fade away as he leaned in, and their lips met in a soft, intimate kiss.

It was a kiss filled with promise and the beginning of something new. When they finally pulled away, they both smiled, feeling a sense of connection that went beyond words.

Chapter 7: A New Perspective

Liam sat at the kitchen table, the comforting aroma of freshly brewed coffee filling the air. The sun had just begun its ascent, casting a warm glow through the windows of Aunt Kim's cozy kitchen. It was a familiar setting, one that had always provided solace and clarity.

Aunt Kim bustled around, preparing breakfast with her usual efficiency. She paused to look at Liam, noticing the thoughtful expression on his face. "You seem deep in thought this morning, Liam," she said, her voice gentle and inviting.

Liam smiled softly, grateful for his aunt's perceptiveness. "Yeah, I've got a lot on my mind," he admitted. As he stared into his coffee, Liam's thoughts swirled. "How do I even begin to explain what I'm feeling?" He wondered. "Ellie... she's more than just a friend. Every moment with her feels like a gift."

Kim set a plate of toast and eggs in front of him before sitting down with her cup of coffee. "Want to talk about it? You know I'm always here to listen."

Taking a sip of his coffee, Liam considered his words carefully. "It's about Ellie," he began, feeling a warmth spread through him at the mere mention of her name. "I've been spending a lot of time with her lately, and...I think I'm developing feelings for her."

Kim's eyes sparkled with curiosity. "Tell me more about Ellie. What is it about her that's caught your heart?"

Liam leaned back in his chair, thinking about the past few weeks. "She's incredible, Aunt Kim. She's passionate about photography, and she has this amazing way of seeing beauty in everything. Being around her makes me feel...alive, in a way I haven't felt in a long time."

Kim smiled, her expression warm and understanding. "It sounds like she's brought a lot of light into your life."

"She has," Liam agreed, his thoughts drifting back to their shared moments. "But it's more than that. She's been through a lot, just like me. And despite her struggles, she's so strong and resilient. I admire that about her."

Kim reached across the table to give his hand a reassuring squeeze. "It sounds like you've found someone special, Liam. Don't let fear hold you back. Sometimes, the best things in life come when we take a leap of faith."

Liam nodded, feeling a sense of clarity and determination. She's right, he thought. I've been so focused on the villa that I've forgotten to enjoy life. Maybe spending time with Elara will be the balance I need. "You're right. I don't want to let this opportunity slip away. I think…I think I'm ready to see where things go with Ellie."

Kim's smile widened. "That's the spirit. And remember, no matter what happens, you have a family that loves and supports you."

Liam felt a wave of gratitude wash over him. "Thanks, Aunt Kim. Your support means the world to me."

Kim took a sip of her coffee and then added, "You know, Liam, you've been working so hard on this renovation. Maybe it's time to take a little break. Spend some time enjoying yourself and the beauty of Isla del Sol. It could do you good."

Liam considered her words, realizing the truth in them. "You're right. I've been so focused on the villa that I've barely taken any time for myself. Maybe spending some time with Ellie, exploring the island, would be just what I need."

Kim nodded approvingly. "Exactly. The work will still be here when you get back, but these moments of joy and connection. They're fleeting. Embrace them while you can."

She paused, her expression turning thoughtful. "You know, your father, my brother, sometimes forgets that all work and no play can catch up with you. But you're learning that now, Liam, and it's something that will help you grow and move the company forward in ways he might not have considered. It's a good life lesson to find that work-home balance. And finding someone you want to share it with is equally important."

Liam felt a newfound sense of understanding. "You're right, Aunt Kim. Balancing work and life is important. I need to take that to heart, not just for myself, but for the future of the business too."

As Liam reflected on Aunt Kim's words, a realization dawned on him. Perhaps his trip to Isla del Sol wasn't a punishment after all, but a teaching lesson meant to better himself. The picturesque island wasn't just an escape—it was a reminder of the life he wanted to build and the balance he needed to maintain.

As they finished their breakfast, Liam felt a renewed sense of purpose. He was ready to embrace the possibilities that lay ahead, both with the villa's renovation and his blossoming relationship with Elara. The island of Isla del Sol had already worked its magic, and he was eager to see what the future held.

Across the way, Elara sat on her villa's veranda, a steaming cup of coffee in her hands. The early morning light filtered through the palm trees, casting dappled shadows on the wooden floor. She took a sip, savoring the rich flavor, and let her thoughts wander.

The past couple weeks had been transformative. Isla del Sol had a way of soothing her soul, and the island's beauty had reignited her passion for photography. Each day brought new inspirations and new perspectives.

But it wasn't just the island that had touched her heart. Liam had become an unexpected source of joy and comfort. *I didn't come here looking for love,* Elara mused, *but Liam... he's different. He makes me feel alive; in a way I haven't felt in so long.* She found herself looking forward to their time together, feeling a connection that was both exciting and a little scary.

As she gazed out at the ocean, Elara thought about her journey to this point. Her breakup with Daniel had been painful, shaking her confidence and making her question her path. Daniel's words used to haunt me, she thought, but now they feel like echoes of a distant past. And Professor Hayes... Elara sighed; his critiques no longer hold power over me. I'm rediscovering who I am and what I love.

But here, on this serene island, those doubts and fears were beginning to fade. She was rediscovering her confidence and her love for photography. And Liam's presence was a big part of that healing process. Her heart pitter-pattered at the thought of him, and butterflies danced in her stomach—a feeling she hadn't expected or planned for when she came to Isla del Sol. It hit her that there might be more to her feelings for Liam than just friendship.

Elara set her coffee cup down and picked up her camera, feeling a surge of determination. She wanted to capture this moment, this feeling of hope and renewal. As she framed the shot, she focused on the vibrant sunrise casting a golden glow over the island. The waves gently kissed the shore, and the palm trees swayed gracefully in the morning breeze. It was a picture-perfect moment that symbolized a new beginning, not just for the day but for her spirit as well. She couldn't help but smile, thinking of the day ahead and the possibilities it held.

Just then, a knock on her door pulled her from her thoughts. She opened it to find Liam standing there, his smile warm and inviting. "Hey, Liam! What brings you here?"

Liam returned her smile, feeling a rush of warmth. "Hey, Ellie. I was wondering if you'd like to take a break from everything and explore the island with me. Aunt Kim suggested I take some time off to enjoy myself, and I can't think of a better way to do that than spending time with you."

Elara's eyes sparkled with excitement. "That sounds amazing, Liam. I'd love to explore the island with you."

With that, they set off on their adventure. The island of Isla del Sol was a paradise of hidden gems waiting to be discovered. They wandered through lush forests, visited secluded beaches, and marveled at the vibrant flora and fauna that surrounded them.

At one point, they found themselves at a small, hidden waterfall. The sound of the cascading water was soothing, and the pool at the base of the falls was invitingly clear.

"Wow, this place is beautiful," Elara said, snapping a few photos with her camera. "I can't believe we found this."

Liam smiled, feeling a sense of awe. "Isla del Sol never ceases to amaze me. And it's even better experiencing it with you."

They sat by the waterfall, enjoying the tranquil setting. Elara turned to Liam her expression thoughtful. "You know, Liam, this island has a way of bringing out the best in people. It's been helping me rediscover my passion for photography and my confidence. And being here with you...it feels right."

Liam reached out and took her hand, feeling a surge of emotion. "I feel the same way, Ellie. You've brought a lot of light into my life, and I can't thank you enough for that."

As they sat there, hand in hand, the world around them seemed to fade away. They were simply two people, finding solace and joy in each other's company.

Elara's eyes sparkled with an idea. "Let's take a photo together," she suggested, her excitement contagious. "I want to capture this moment." She set up her camera on a nearby rock and adjusted the settings. Using the timer function, Elara quickly joined Liam by the waterfall. *Being with Liam feels so right,* she realized, *I'm not just capturing a memory—I'm capturing a piece of my heart.* As the timer counted down, they both smiled, feeling the thrill of capturing their happiness. *This moment is perfect,* Liam thought, *I want to remember it forever.* The camera clicked, preserving the moment forever.

Liam looked into Elara's eyes, his heart pounding with a mix of excitement and nervousness. He leaned in closer, his breath mingling with hers. Elara's heart raced, and she felt a flutter of anticipation. As their lips met, the kiss was more passionate and lingering than before, filled with unspoken emotions and a deep connection. The sound of the waterfall provided a soothing backdrop, making the moment even more magical.

Just as they were about to leave the waterfall, Liam noticed a barely visible path leading through the dense foliage. "Hey, Ellie, look at this. It looks like an old path. Do you want to see where it leads?"

Elara's curiosity was piqued. "Absolutely. Let's check it out."

They followed the winding path, the air filled with the scent of blooming flowers and the sounds of nature. After a short hike, they emerged from the forest to find themselves standing in front of an old lighthouse.

"Wow," Elara breathed, her eyes wide with wonder. "I had no idea this was here."

As she took in the lighthouse, memories of one of her solo adventures came rushing back. The lighthouse stood tall and proud against the backdrop of the ocean, its weathered stone walls telling stories of days gone by.

"This... this is the lighthouse I saw earlier," she realized, her voice tinged with awe. "I spotted it from afar during one of my walks, but I never got this close."

Liam smiled at her reaction, enjoying the sense of discovery they shared.

"Let's go inside," he suggested, nodding toward the entrance.

Inside, the air was cool and filled with the faint scent of sea salt and aged wood. The spiral staircase beckoned them upward, and they began to climb. With each step, the view outside the small windows became more breathtaking.

At the top, they were greeted by a panoramic view of the island and the endless expanse of ocean. Elara felt a sense of awe and serenity wash over her. She raised her camera to capture the moment, the lens focusing on the horizon where the sky met the sea.

Liam stood beside her, their shoulders touching. "It's incredible, isn't it?" he said softly.

"It's stunning," Elara whispered, snapping photos with her camera. "Thank you for bringing me here, Liam."

Their adventure continued, and with each discovery, their bond grew stronger. They shared stories, laughed, and found themselves opening up to each other in ways they hadn't before. The island's magic seemed to weave their lives together, creating memories that would last a lifetime.

As the sun began to set, casting a golden glow over the island, Liam and Elara found themselves standing on a cliff overlooking the ocean. The view was breathtaking, and the moment felt perfect.

"Look at that sunset," Elara whispered, her voice filled with awe. The sky was ablaze with hues of orange, pink, and purple, reflecting off the shimmering waves below.

Liam wrapped an arm around her shoulders, pulling her close. "It's like the island is putting on a show just for us," he said softly.

They stood in comfortable silence, watching as the sun dipped below the horizon, leaving a trail of colors in its wake. The air was cool, and the sound of the waves crashing against the rocks added a soothing rhythm to the moment.

Elara took out her camera, capturing the stunning view. "I want to remember this forever," she said, her eyes glistening with emotion.

Liam smiled, feeling a profound sense of contentment. "Me too," he replied. "This is one of those moments you never want to end."

As the last rays of sunlight faded, the sky transformed into a deep indigo, and the first stars began to twinkle. Liam and Elara decided to make their way back to the villa, the path illuminated by the soft glow of the moon.

"It's been an unforgettable day," Elara said, her voice filled with gratitude. "Thank you for sharing it with me, Liam."

Liam squeezed her hand, his heart full. "Thank you, Ellie. You've made it special."

They paused for a moment, standing under the starlit sky. Liam looked into Elara's eyes, feeling a surge of emotion. He leaned in, and their lips met in a tender, lingering kiss. The world around them seemed to fade away, leaving only the two of them, lost in the magic of the moment.

Chapter 8: The Secret Beach

Elara woke to the sound of waves gently lapping against the shore and the first light of dawn filtering through her window. The memories of the previous day's adventures with Liam brought a smile to her face. She felt a sense of peace and anticipation for what the new day would bring.

After a quick breakfast, Elara grabbed her camera and headed outside. The island was just beginning to stir, with the scent of blooming flowers in the air and the distant calls of exotic birds. She found Liam waiting by the villa's entrance, his eyes bright with excitement.

"Good morning, Ellie," he greeted with a warm smile. "Ready for another adventure?"

Elara nodded, her heart fluttering at the thought. "Absolutely. What's on the agenda for today?"

Liam winked playfully. "I thought we could explore the hidden coves on the north side of the island. There's supposed to be a secret beach that only the locals know about."

Elara raised an eyebrow, a hint of concern in her voice. "But don't you have to work on the villa today?"

Liam chuckled, shaking his head. "Actually, my aunt insisted I take a couple of days off to enjoy myself. She said I deserve a break and that the villa can manage without me for a bit."

Relieved, Elara smiled. "That sounds perfect. Let's make the most of it."

Curiosity piqued; Elara eagerly followed Liam as they set off down the winding path. They navigated through dense foliage and rocky terrain, the sounds of the jungle surrounding them. With each step, Elara's excitement grew, and she couldn't help but marvel at the island's untouched beauty.

Finally, they emerged from the jungle to find a secluded beach, the golden sand stretching out before them. The turquoise water was crystal clear, and the beach was framed by towering cliffs, creating a hidden paradise.

Elara's eyes sparkled with wonder as she raised her camera. "This is incredible, Liam."

He grinned, watching her with admiration. "I knew you'd love it. Let's make the most of our day here."

As they settled on the secluded beach, Elara and Liam decided to make the most of their time in paradise. They started by taking a refreshing swim in the crystal-clear water, the cool waves providing relief from the warm sun. They laughed and splashed, their playful interactions feeling like two people falling in love. It was as if the ocean itself was drawing them closer together.

While they swam, the world seemed to fade away, leaving just the two of them in their own little bubble. Elara felt the warmth of Liam's presence beside her, and each time their hands brushed against each other in the water, she felt a spark of electricity.

At one point, they floated side by side, gazing up at the azure sky. Liam turned to Elara, his eyes full of admiration. "This feels like a dream," he said softly. "I'm so glad we're here together."

Elara's heart swelled with emotion. She felt an undeniable connection to Liam, something deeper than friendship. "Me too, Liam. It's like everything is just... perfect."

As they drifted in the gentle waves, the distance between them seemed to vanish. Liam reached out and took Elara's hand, his touch sending a shiver of excitement down her spine. "Ellie, there's something about you that makes me feel alive," he confessed, his voice full of sincerity.

Elara's breath caught in her throat as she met his gaze. "I feel the same way, Liam. Being with you feels like the most natural thing in the world."

For a moment, they floated in silence, their fingers intertwined, letting the water cradle them. It was a simple yet profound moment, one that felt like two people in love discovering a new world together. The ocean, the island, and the gentle rhythm of the waves all seemed to conspire to bring them closer.

Reluctantly, they swam back to the shore, but the bond they had felt in the water lingered in the air. Their hearts were lighter, and the connection between them had deepened in a way neither could deny.

After their swim, they laid out a blanket on the soft sand and enjoyed a picnic they had packed. The taste of fresh fruit, sandwiches, and cold drinks was even better with the stunning view of the turquoise ocean. They chatted and shared stories, their bond growing stronger with each passing moment.

Liam leaned back on the blanket, gazing out at the horizon with a wistful smile. "You know, Ellie, this island holds a lot of memories for me. When I was a kid, my parents used to bring my older brother and me here to visit my aunt. We spent our summers exploring every inch of this place."

Elara looked at him, intrigued. "That sounds amazing. What was it like?"

Liam's eyes lit up with nostalgia. "It was like a paradise for two adventurous boys. My brother, Ethan, and I would spend hours building sandcastles, snorkeling, and pretending we were pirates searching for hidden treasure. My aunt always had the most incredible stories about the island's history and legends. We even tried to find the secret beach a few times but never succeeded."

Elara smiled warmly, imagining a young Liam and his brother on their adventures. "Did your brother ever come back here after those summers?"

Liam's expression grew more serious, but with a touch of warmth. "Not really. As we grew older, life got busier. Ethan went off to medical school and became a doctor. He's always been the ambitious one. My dad was planning to retire and move back to the island, but my mom passed away, and it changed everything. My dad handed over the business to me just before I got sent to the villa. He said it was time for me to take charge and make something of it."

Elara reached out and gently squeezed his hand. "I'm sorry, Liam. It must be hard not having your mom around."

Liam nodded, his gaze softening as he looked at her. "It is, but being here with you brings back all those good memories. It feels like I'm reconnecting with a part of my past that I've missed."

Elara felt a surge of affection for Liam, touched by his vulnerability. "I'm glad we can create new memories together. And who knows, maybe we'll find that secret beach today."

Liam's smile returned, brighter than ever. "I think we already have. This moment right here feels like a hidden treasure."

They shared a comfortable silence for a while, simply enjoying each other's company. After a few moments, Liam turned to Elara with curiosity in his eyes. "Ellie, I've always wanted to ask – what got you into photography?"

Elara's face lit up as she began to speak. "It started when I was a teenager. My grandfather gave me my first camera. He was an avid photographer himself, always capturing moments of beauty and everyday life. When he passed away, I inherited his camera. It felt like a way to keep his memory alive and stay connected to him."

Liam listened intently, his admiration for Elara growing. "That's a beautiful reason. I can see how much it means to you."

Elara nodded, a soft smile playing on her lips. "Photography became a way for me to express myself and capture the world around me. It helps me see things differently, find beauty in the mundane, and preserve memories. It's like telling a story through images."

Liam's eyes sparkled with appreciation. "I can see that passion in your photos. They have a way of capturing the essence of a moment, the emotions behind it."

Elara blushed slightly, feeling a warm glow from his words. "Thank you, Liam. That means a lot coming from you."

Liam reached out and gently tucked a strand of hair behind her ear. "I'm glad you're here with me, Ellie. Today feels like one of those moments worth capturing and holding onto."

Elara's heart fluttered at his touch, and she felt an even deeper connection to him. "I feel the same way. Let's make sure we have plenty more moments like this."

As the afternoon sun climbed higher, they lounged on the beach, soaking up the sun's warmth. Elara captured the beauty of the day with her camera, while Liam dozed off, the gentle sound of the waves lulling him into a peaceful nap. She couldn't resist taking a few candid shots of him, his relaxed expression a testament to the day's perfect serenity. His tousled hair and the way the sunlight kissed his skin made for the most endearing photos she'd taken in a long time.

As she lowered her camera, Elara felt a surge of affection for Liam. Watching him so peaceful and content, she realized just how much he meant to her. It wasn't just friendship; it was something deeper, something that felt like he was meant to be in her life. The feeling of love washed over her like a gentle wave, filling her heart with warmth and certainty. The urge to kiss him was almost overwhelming, but she hesitated, not wanting to disturb his rest.

Meanwhile, as they spent the day together, Liam found himself increasingly captivated by Elara. Her laughter was infectious, her curiosity boundless, and her passion for capturing the beauty around them was inspiring. Watching her through the lens of her camera, he saw not just the stunning island landscapes but the light in her eyes and the warmth of her smile. Each moment they shared brought him closer to realizing that his feelings for her were growing stronger. It wasn't just admiration or friendship; it was something deeper. He felt a protective instinct and a profound connection, as if she was meant to be a part of his life. The realization filled him with a mixture of excitement and vulnerability, knowing that he was falling in love with her. As the sun set and they stood on the beach, he felt a sense of contentment and hope for the future, wishing for more days like this, side by side with Elara.

Later, they explored the rocky tide pools, marveling at the colorful marine life. Tiny fish darted between the rocks, and sea anemones swayed gently with the water's movement. Elara couldn't resist capturing these moments, feeling inspired by the island's natural wonders.

By the time the sun began to set, casting a golden glow over the beach, they were back on their blanket, watching the sky transform into a canvas of vibrant colors. Elara leaned her head on Liam's shoulder, feeling content and grateful for the unforgettable day they had shared.

"I don't want this to end," Elara whispered, her voice filled with emotion. "Today has been perfect, and I wish we could stay like this forever."

Liam turned his head slightly to look at her, his eyes reflecting the same sentiment. "I feel the same way, Ellie. Being here with you makes everything feel right. I don't want it to end either."

Elara smiled, her heart swelling with warmth. "It's like we've found our own little paradise."

Liam nodded, gently placing his arm around her. "We have. And I want to have many more days like this with you."

Elara felt a surge of happiness at his words, knowing that their connection was mutual and strong. "Me too, Liam. Let's make sure we create more moments like this, together."

As they sat there, watching the sky's vibrant hues, they both felt a profound sense of contentment and hope for the future. The bond they had forged during the day was undeniable, and the promise of more shared adventures filled them with joy.

Elara turned to face Liam; her eyes filled with emotion. "Liam, there's something I've been wanting to do all day."

Liam's gaze locked with hers, his heart pounding. "What is it, Ellie?"

Without another word, Elara leaned in and gently pressed her lips to his. The kiss was soft and sweet, filled with the promise of everything they had yet to discover together. Liam responded, wrapping his arms around her and deepening the kiss, both of them lost in the moment.

When they finally pulled away, Elara's cheeks were flushed, and her heart was racing. "I've wanted to do that for a while," she admitted, her voice barely above a whisper.

Liam smiled, his eyes shining with affection. "So, have I. That was... perfect."

Elara took a deep breath, feeling a mix of excitement and nervousness. "Liam, would you like to spend the night at my villa? We don't have to end this perfect day just yet."

Liam's expression softened, and he nodded. "I'd love to, Ellie. Spending more time with you sounds like the best idea."

Hand in hand, they made their way back to the villa, the warmth of their shared kiss and the promise of a night together filling them with happiness and anticipation.

Chapter 9: Sunset Encounters

The first light of dawn crept into the villa, casting a gentle glow over the room. Elara stirred, slowly waking from a restful sleep. For a moment, she couldn't quite place where she was, but then the events of the previous day came flooding back, filling her with warmth and a sense of contentment.

As she turned her head and found Liam sleeping peacefully beside her, she couldn't help but think about how natural it felt to have him there. Was it possible that their connection was growing stronger than she had ever imagined?

Quietly, Elara slipped out of bed, careful not to wake Liam. She padded softly to the kitchen and started brewing coffee, the rich aroma filling the air. As she waited for the coffee to be ready, she glanced out the window at the island awakening to a new day, feeling a sense of anticipation for whatever lay ahead.

Liam awoke to the smell of coffee and the sight of Elara, her hair cascading over her shoulders as she stood by the window. He watched her for a moment, feeling a deep sense of peace and happiness. He realized that being with Elara made everything feel right. It was as if she brought a sense of completeness to his life that he hadn't even known was missing.

"Good morning, Ellie," he said softly, his voice still heavy with sleep.

Elara turned to him, her smile lighting up the room. "Good morning, Liam. Did you sleep well?"

Liam nodded, stretching and sitting up. "Better than I have in a long time. Yesterday was amazing, Ellie. Thank you."

Elara's heart fluttered at his words. "It was perfect, wasn't it? I feel so lucky to have you here with me."

They shared a quiet moment, the connection between them growing stronger with each passing second. As Liam got out of bed and joined Elara by the window, he couldn't shake the feeling that this was where he belonged—right here, by her side.

"I have an idea," Liam said, his voice filled with excitement. "How about we spend the morning together exploring more of the island? There are still so many hidden gems we haven't discovered yet."

Elara's eyes sparkled with enthusiasm but then softened with a hint of practicality. "I'd love that, Liam. Let's enjoy the morning together, and then in the afternoon, you can get back to work on the villa. While you're working, I'll prepare us a nice meal for the evening."

Liam smiled, appreciating her thoughtfulness. "That sounds like a perfect plan, Ellie. We'll get the best of both worlds."

Hand in hand, they stepped out into the morning light, ready to embrace the day ahead. The island awaited, and with it, the promise of new memories and deepening feelings.

They decided to explore deeper into the jungle, away from the familiar paths and the shoreline. The dense foliage enveloped them, and the sounds of the jungle—chirping birds, rustling leaves, and distant animal calls—created an enchanting symphony. Liam led the way, guiding Elara through the thick underbrush and around towering trees. As they ventured further, Elara marveled at the vibrant colors and the rich diversity of plant life. She stopped frequently to capture the beauty with her camera, her eyes alight with wonder.

"Look at these flowers, Liam," Elara exclaimed, pointing to a cluster of bright, exotic blooms. "I've never seen anything like them."

Liam grinned, enjoying her excitement. "This island is full of surprises. There's so much beauty hidden in every corner." He looked into her eyes, his expression softening with affection. In that moment, he felt an overwhelming urge to kiss her, to show her just how much she meant to him.

Without thinking, Elara closed the distance between them and pressed her lips to his. The kiss was gentle and sweet, a perfect reflection of their growing feelings. When they pulled away, they both smiled, feeling an even deeper connection.

"I'm so glad we're doing this together," Elara whispered, her voice full of emotion.

Liam nodded, his gaze warm and tender. "Me too, Ellie. This feels like a dream."

As they continued their exploration, Elara's attention was drawn to the vibrant tropical birds flitting through the trees. Their feathers displayed an array of dazzling colors—brilliant blues, fiery reds, sunny yellows, and deep greens. She couldn't contain her excitement as she captured their beauty with her camera.

"Look at these birds, Liam!" Elara exclaimed; her voice filled with awe. "They're so beautiful and colorful. It's like the jungle is alive with magic."

Liam smiled, watching her with admiration. He was amazed by how she could find wonder in everything, how her passion for life made everything seem brighter. Being with her was like seeing the world through new eyes.

Elara's heart swelled with joy as she watched a pair of bright blue parrots fluttering overhead. "I could spend hours just photographing them. Their colors are so vivid, and they move with such grace."

Liam chuckled, his gaze never leaving her. "Your excitement is contagious, Ellie. I feel like I'm seeing the island in a whole new light, thanks to you."

As the sun climbed higher in the sky, signaling the approach of noon, Elara and Liam decided to head back to the villa. The morning had been filled with exploration and excitement, and they both felt a sense of accomplishment and connection.

"That was incredible," Elara said, her eyes still bright with wonder from their jungle adventure. "I can't wait to see how the photos turn out."

Liam smiled, gently squeezing her hand as they walked. "I'm sure they'll be amazing, just like you."

They made their way back through the jungle, eventually emerging onto the familiar path leading to the villa. The scent of blooming flowers filled the air, and the distant sound of waves added a soothing backdrop to their journey.

Once they reached the villa, Elara began preparing a light lunch while Liam washed up. She put together a simple yet delicious meal of fresh fruit, salads, and sandwiches. The aroma of freshly cut herbs and the vibrant colors of the ingredients added to the sense of contentment that had marked their day so far.

Liam joined her in the kitchen, helping to set the table on the veranda overlooking the ocean. They enjoyed their meal together, the conversation flowing easily as they recounted their morning's discoveries and shared stories from their lives.

"This has been such a perfect day," Elara said, taking a sip of her drink. "I'm glad we got to explore the jungle together."

Liam nodded, his eyes reflecting his happiness. "Me too, Ellie. It's been unforgettable."

As they finished their lunch, Liam stretched and stood up. "I should get started on the villa. There's still a lot of work to be done."

Elara smiled and kissed his cheek. "I'll head to the local market to pick up some ingredients for our dinner. I might even learn a new recipe or two."

Liam smiled, appreciating her thoughtfulness. "That sounds like a great idea. I'll see you later this afternoon."

Elara grabbed her bag and camera, heading to the bustling local market she had visited on her arrival. The market was alive with vibrant colors, enticing aromas, and the lively chatter of vendors and customers. She strolled through the stalls, admiring the fresh produce, fragrant spices, and handmade crafts.

As she explored, her eyes were drawn to a stall run by a friendly-looking woman named Rosa, who was selling an array of fresh vegetables and herbs. Elara approached with a smile, intrigued by the variety of ingredients.

"Hello," Elara greeted, her curiosity evident. "Everything looks so fresh and delicious. I'm planning to make a special dinner tonight and was wondering if you had any suggestions."

Rosa's eyes twinkled with warmth as she welcomed Elara. "Of course! I'm Rosa. I have a wonderful recipe for a traditional island dish called 'Camarones a la Isla'—island-style shrimp. Would you like to learn how to make it?"

Elara's excitement was palpable. "Yes, I'd love to! Thank you, Rosa."

Rosa guided Elara through the ingredients, explaining each one with care. They picked out fresh shrimp, garlic, tomatoes, peppers, and a mix of local herbs and spices. As they gathered the ingredients, Rosa shared stories about the island and its culinary traditions, making the experience even more special.

Back at the stall, Rosa demonstrated how to prepare the dish, and Elara took notes, eager to recreate it later. The process was a delightful blend of chopping, sautéing, and seasoning, resulting in a fragrant and flavorful dish that Elara couldn't wait to share with Liam.

"This looks amazing, Rosa. Thank you so much for teaching me," Elara said, her gratitude evident.

Rosa smiled warmly. "It was my pleasure, Elara. I hope you and Liam enjoy it."

With her bag filled with fresh ingredients and new knowledge, Elara made her way back to the villa, feeling inspired and excited for the evening ahead. As she walked, she couldn't help but think about how Liam would react to the special meal she had prepared for him. She wanted to create a moment that would bring them even closer together.

Back at the villa, Elara saw Liam working next door and couldn't resist the urge to capture some candid shots of him. She watched from a distance as he repaired a few broken tiles on the roof, repainted the shutters, and tended to the garden. Her heart swelled with admiration for his dedication and hard work.

As she clicked the shutter, she thought about how much he had come to mean to her. In these quiet moments, she realized just how deeply she cared for him and how much she wanted to be a part of his life.

Satisfied with the photos, Elara returned to her villa and began preparing dinner. She selected fresh ingredients, experimenting with flavors and creating a menu that reflected the island's bounty. The kitchen soon filled with the enticing aroma of spices and herbs, promising a delightful meal to end their day.

As the sun began to set, casting a golden glow over the island, Liam returned to Elara's villa. He looked tired but satisfied with the progress he had made. Elara greeted him with a warm smile and a kiss.

"Welcome back," she said, her voice filled with affection. "Dinner is almost ready. I learned a new recipe today, and I can't wait for you to try it." Liam took a deep breath, savoring the delicious smells wafting from the kitchen. "It smells amazing, Ellie. I can't wait to try it."

They set the table on the veranda, the ocean providing a beautiful backdrop for their meal. The gentle rustle of palm leaves swayed in harmony with the whispering ocean breeze, carrying the faint scent of salt and tropical flowers. Soft island music played in the background, the gentle melodies blending seamlessly with the sound of the waves. The ambiance was perfect, creating a sense of tranquility and romance.

As they enjoyed their dinner, the conversation flowed easily, filled with laughter and shared dreams. The flavors of the island's spices danced on their tongues, mingling with the sweetness of ripe mangoes and the savory aroma of grilled shrimp. The bond between them grew stronger with each passing moment, making the day truly unforgettable.

As the moon rose over the horizon, casting its glow on the waters, the shimmering reflections danced in anticipation of what the night would bring to the new lovers. Elara and Liam leaned closer, their eyes reflecting the moonlight and the promise of a deepening connection. "This is perfect," Elara whispered, her voice soft and filled with emotion. "I couldn't have imagined a more wonderful evening." Liam's hand found hers, their fingers intertwining. "It is perfect, Ellie. Being here with you, sharing this moment, it feels like a dream."

They sat in companionable silence for a while, simply enjoying the beauty of the night and the warmth of each other's presence. The soft music, the moonlit ocean, and the gentle sounds of the island created an enchanting atmosphere that wrapped around them like a warm embrace.

Elara could feel the warmth of Liam's hand, roughened from his day's work, yet tender as it held hers. Her mind wandered to the ticking clock—her time on the island was quickly winding down. She couldn't bring herself to speak about it, not wanting to taint the magic of the moment with the impending reality of their separation. Elara felt her heart swell with happiness as she looked at Liam. "Let's promise to always cherish moments like these, no matter what the future holds."

Liam nodded, his eyes filled with love and sincerity. "I promise, Ellie. We'll make every moment count."

The night was filled with the magic of new beginnings, and as they sat together, they knew that their journey had only just begun.

Chapter 10: Shared Moments

Two weeks had passed since that magical evening on the veranda, and Elara and Liam had grown even closer. Their days were filled with exploration and discovery, each moment strengthening their bond. However, the looming reality of Elara's departure was never far from their minds.

One afternoon, Liam found himself in the cozy kitchen of his Aunt Kim's cottage, helping her prepare a batch of her famous island cookies. The scent of vanilla and spices filled the air, creating a comforting atmosphere. As Liam worked, Aunt Kim observed him with a knowing look.

"You've been spending a lot of time with Elara," she remarked gently, her tone filled with warmth.

Liam looked up, surprised by her comment but not entirely caught off guard. He nodded, a small smile playing on his lips. "Yeah, Aunt Kim. She's...she's incredible. Being with her feels so natural, like I've known her forever."

Aunt Kim continued mixing the ingredients, her hands deft and experienced. "I can see that, dear. It's written all over your face. But you know, the island isn't forever. Elara will be leaving soon."

Liam's expression clouded for a moment, the reality of her words sinking in. He sighed, leaning against the counter. "I know. And that's what scares me. I don't want to lose what we have, Aunt Kim. It feels too important."

Aunt Kim paused, turning to face him. Her eyes were filled with understanding and compassion. "Love is a beautiful thing, Liam, but it also requires courage. You have to be willing to take risks, to follow your heart even when it seems uncertain."

Liam nodded, taking her words to heart. "I care about her so much, Aunt Kim. I just don't know what's going to happen when she leaves."

Aunt Kim reached out and placed a comforting hand on his shoulder. "Whatever happens, Liam, you'll find a way. If it's meant to be, you'll make it work. Just remember to cherish every moment you have together."

As they continued baking, Liam felt a renewed sense of determination. He knew that the time he had with Elara was precious, and he was resolved to make the most of it, no matter what the future held.

Later that evening, as they finished their cookies, Liam turned to his aunt with a hopeful look. "Aunt Kim, I want to do something special for Elara before she leaves. Would you help me set up a romantic dinner for her?"

Aunt Kim's eyes sparkled with delight. "Of course, dear! I'd love to help. What do you have in mind?"

Liam smiled, feeling a sense of excitement. "I was thinking we could set up a candlelit dinner on the beach. With some of your amazing cooking, of course."

Aunt Kim chuckled, patting his hand. "That sounds like a wonderful idea, Liam. We'll make it a night to remember."

As the sun dipped lower in the sky, Aunt Kim and Liam busied themselves with preparations. They set up a small table on the beach, adorned with a simple yet elegant white tablecloth and delicate candles. Fairy lights were strung along the nearby trees, casting a soft, magical glow over the area. Aunt Kim prepared a delicious meal featuring fresh seafood, tropical fruits, and some of her signature island dishes.

Meanwhile, on the other side of the island, Elara sat on the beach, her toes buried in the warm sand. The gentle lapping of the waves provided a soothing rhythm as she gazed out at the horizon. She held her camera in her lap, flipping through the photos she had taken over the past two weeks.

Each image brought back a flood of memories—the vibrant colors of the jungle, the playful tropical birds, the serene sunsets they had watched together. But it was the candid shots of Liam that made her heart ache with a mixture of joy and sadness.

She thought about how much he had come to mean to her, how his presence had filled her days with laughter and a sense of belonging. Elara knew that her time on the island was running out, and the thought of leaving Liam behind felt like a heavy weight on her chest.

She sighed, her thoughts drifting back to their first meeting. It was as if fate had brought them together, and now, the idea of parting seemed unbearable. Elara wondered what would happen once she left the island. Would their connection fade away, or could they find a way to make it work despite the distance?

As the sun began to set, casting a golden glow over the water, Elara made a silent promise to herself. She would cherish every remaining moment with Liam and hold onto the hope that their bond would endure, no matter where life took them.

With renewed determination, she stood up and made her way back to the villa. There was still so much she wanted to share with Liam, and she wasn't ready to let go just yet.

Back at the villa, Liam was putting the finishing touches on the dinner setup. He placed a bouquet of freshly picked flowers on the table, their vibrant colors adding to the romantic ambiance. As he stepped back to admire their work, Aunt Kim gave him an approving nod.

"This looks perfect, Liam. Elara is going to love it," she said with a smile.

Liam's heart swelled with anticipation. "I hope so, Aunt Kim. I really want this night to be special for her."

Just then, Elara appeared on the path leading to the beach, her eyes widening in surprise as she took in the scene. The fairy lights twinkled in the growing dusk, and the scent of the delicious meal wafted through the air.

"Liam, what is all this?" she asked, her voice filled with wonder.

Liam walked over to her, taking her hand and leading her to the table. "I wanted to do something special for you, Ellie. You've made my time here unforgettable, and I wanted to show you how much you mean to me."

Tears of joy filled Elara's eyes as she looked at him, her heart overflowing with emotion. "This is amazing, Liam. Thank you."

They sat down to enjoy the meal, the sound of the waves providing a soothing backdrop to their conversation. The evening was filled with laughter, heartfelt words, and the magic of the island. As the night grew darker, the connection between them deepened.

After they finished their meal, Liam stood up and reached into his pocket, pulling out a small velvet box. "Elara, I have something for you," he said, his voice tinged with nervousness and excitement.

Elara looked at him with curiosity and anticipation as he opened the box to reveal a delicate necklace. The pendant was a beautifully crafted seashell, encrusted with tiny, shimmering gems that caught the light and sparkled like the ocean waves.

"This necklace belonged to my grandmother," Liam explained, his voice filled with emotion. "She gave it to my mom, and then my mom passed it on to me. It's always been a symbol of love and connection in our family. I want you to have it, Ellie, as a reminder of our time together and the bond we share."

Tears welled up in Elara's eyes as she looked at the necklace and then back at Liam. "Liam, this is so beautiful and meaningful. I don't know what to say."

Liam smiled, gently placing the necklace around her neck. "You don't have to say anything, Ellie. Just know that you mean the world to me."

Elara touched the pendant, feeling its warmth against her skin. "I'll cherish this always, Liam. Thank you."

Liam held her gaze, his eyes filled with sincerity. "And remember, this doesn't have to end. Our connection is meant to be."

A tear fell down her face, glistening in the moonlight. It was a happy and sad moment. She knew she was leaving the island tomorrow afternoon, but she had fallen in love with Liam and she had to tell him. Elara took a deep breath, steadying herself as she looked into Liam's eyes. "Liam," she began, her voice trembling with emotion, "I've fallen in love with you. These past weeks have been the most amazing of my life, and I can't imagine leaving without telling you how I feel."

Liam's eyes widened with surprise, his heart racing. He reached out, gently wiping the tear from her cheek. "Ellie, I've fallen in love with you too. I don't want this to end. I want us to find a way to be together, no matter what."

Elara felt a rush of relief and joy at his words. "Do you really mean that, Liam? Can we make this work, even after I leave?"

Liam nodded; his gaze filled with determination. "We'll find a way, Ellie. Our connection is special, and it's meant to be. We'll make every moment count and cherish this love we've found."

Elara smiled, feeling a sense of hope. "You know, you're not the only one facing changes. I'll be leaving tomorrow, but you'll be leaving the island soon too, right?"

Liam nodded, his expression turning serious. "Yes, I have to go back home and try to take back control of the family business that my father wrested from me. It's going to be a tough journey, but knowing you're with me in spirit will give me the strength I need."

Elara squeezed his hand, her eyes filled with warmth and support. "We'll support each other, Liam. No matter where we are, our bond will keep us connected."

Liam took a deep breath, thinking about their future. "We can call and video chat every day," he suggested. "We'll share our lives, our challenges, and our successes. I can visit you whenever I have the chance, and you can come visit me too. We'll make it work, Ellie."

Elara nodded, feeling reassured. "And we'll write letters," she added. "There's something special about holding a letter in your hands and reading the words of someone you love. It will be like a piece of you is with me."

Liam smiled, loving the idea. "I like that. We'll write letters and keep our connection strong. And besides, we're only a five-hour drive apart. It's worth it to make it work with you, Ellie."

Elara looked into his eyes, her heart full of love and determination. "Liam, I believe in us. I believe that we can make this work, no matter what. Our love is worth fighting for."

Liam held her close, feeling the strength of their bond. "I believe in us too, Ellie. We'll face whatever challenges come our way, and we'll come out stronger. Our connection is meant to be."

As they stood together under the stars, the necklace gleaming in the moonlight, they both knew that their journey was only just beginning. They would face their challenges with hope and courage, holding onto the love that had brought them together.

Chapter 11: Leaving Paradise

The time had come for Elara to leave the island and return to her life in the states. As the sun climbed higher in the sky, casting a warm glow over the island, she and Liam shared a final embrace on the beach, their hearts heavy with the impending separation.

Liam looked into her eyes; his voice steady but filled with emotion. "Remember, Ellie, this is not goodbye. It's just the beginning of a new chapter for us. We'll make this work, no matter what."

Elara nodded, her eyes glistening with tears. "I know, Liam. I believe in us. Our love is strong, and we'll find a way to be together."

With a deep breath, Elara turned and walked towards her rental car, parked nearby. Liam followed her, their hands clasped tightly until the last possible moment. As she reached the car, she took one last look at him, etching his image into her memory.

"I'll miss you every day," she whispered, her voice trembling.

"I'll miss you too, Ellie. Drive safe, and call me when you land," Liam replied, his eyes never leaving hers.

Elara started the car and glanced in the rearview mirror. Liam stood on the beach, becoming a distant silhouette against the setting sun. Her heart ached with each passing second until she couldn't bear it any longer. Slamming the brakes, she spun the car around and raced back to him.

"Liam!" she called out, breathless as she ran towards him. She held out her journal. "Take this. It's my journal of our time on the island. So, you'll always have a piece of me with you." Her hand tightened around the necklace she wore. "I love you."

Liam's eyes softened with a bittersweet smile. "Thank you, Ellie. I love you too." Holding the journal close, he felt a small but comforting weight lift from his heart.

As Elara got back into the car, the road ahead appeared both familiar and foreign—a path promising new beginnings but shadowed by the sorrow of leaving her love behind.

The drive to the airport was a blur of emotions. Elara's mind raced with thoughts of their time together, the adventures they had shared, and the bond they had formed. She knew that this was not the end of their story, but rather the start of a new and challenging chapter.

Upon reaching the airport, Elara returned the rental car and made her way to the departure gate. The bustling terminal was a stark contrast to the serene island she had just left, a reminder of the busy life she was returning to. As she checked in and went through security, she held onto the memory of Liam's reassuring words.

Finally, as she boarded the plane and found her seat, Elara took a deep breath, feeling a mixture of sadness and hope. She pulled out her phone and sent a message to Liam, expressing her love and determination to make their relationship work. Each word brought a smile to her face and strengthened her resolve to make their love work, no matter the distance.

As the plane took off, soaring into the sky, Elara looked out the window, watching the island fade into the distance. She knew that their journey was far from over and that they would face the challenges ahead with hope and courage.

Elara had come to Isla del Sol in search of herself, seeking answers to her life's purpose and her passion for photography. What she found was more than she had ever imagined—a renewed sense of purpose, a deeper appreciation for the art she loved, and an unexpected love that had changed her life forever.

With Elara's departure, Liam felt a void that was difficult to fill. The island seemed quieter, and the days felt longer without her presence.

Determined not to let the sadness overwhelm him, he decided to throw himself back into the renovation of the villa, a project that had been close to his heart.

Early each morning, Liam would rise with the sun, ready to tackle the day's tasks. He found solace in the physical work, using it as a way to channel his emotions and keep his mind occupied. The villa, once a symbol of his family's legacy, now became a beacon of hope and renewal.

Liam worked tirelessly, restoring the old structure to its former glory. From repairing the wooden beams to repainting the walls in vibrant island colors, every task reminded him of the life he was building for himself and the promise he had made to Elara. The renovation became a metaphor for his journey—an effort to rebuild not only the villa but also his sense of purpose and direction.

Aunt Kim often stopped by to check on Liam's progress and offer her moral support. During these visits, they would sit together on the veranda, enjoying a cup of tea and sharing heartfelt conversations.

"You're doing a wonderful job, Liam," Aunt Kim would say, her eyes filled with pride. "Your dedication is inspiring."

Liam would smile, his thoughts drifting to Elara. "It's not just about the villa, Aunt Kim. It's about proving to myself that I can make a difference, that I can create something meaningful."

Aunt Kim would nod in understanding. "I know it's been hard since Elara left, but you're turning that pain into something beautiful. She's proud of you, Liam. I can see it in the way you talk about her."

Their conversations became a source of comfort for Liam, helping him navigate the emotional journey of rebuilding both the villa and his own sense of purpose.

Soon the villa began to take shape. The once-outdated building now stood as a testament to Liam's hard work and determination. He transformed the rooms into inviting spaces filled with natural light and island charm. The kitchen, now renovated with modern appliances while retaining its cozy, rustic feel would soon be ready for guests to stay and enjoy their time on Isla del Sol like he had.

Each evening, as he sat on the veranda, Liam would think of Elara. He would picture her smile, hear her laughter, and feel her presence in the memories they had created together. He kept her journal close, often reading through the entries she had written, each word a reminder of their connection.

One day, as Liam was working on the garden, his phone buzzed with a message from Elara. Her words brought a smile to his face, renewing his sense of hope and determination. "Hey Liam, just wanted to let you know that I'm thinking of you. The photos from the island are amazing, and I'm working on a new project inspired by our time together. Can't wait to share it with you."

Liam's heart swelled with pride and love. He replied, "I'm so glad to hear that, Ellie. The villa is coming along beautifully, and I can't wait to show you when you visit. Our bond keeps me going every day."

As he put his phone away, Liam felt a renewed sense of purpose. He was not only rebuilding the villa but also building a future filled with promise and love. The challenges ahead no longer seemed daunting, and he knew that with Elara in his life, no matter the distance, they could overcome anything.

A week later, the villa stood proudly as a testament to Liam's hard work and dedication. The once-outdated structure had been transformed into a beautiful, inviting space, filled with the charm and warmth of the island. Each room now radiated a sense of renewal and hope, reflecting the journey Liam had undertaken both inside and out.

Liam surveyed the villa with a sense of accomplishment. The vibrant island colors on the walls, the polished wooden beams, and the cozy, modern kitchen were all reminders of the countless hours he had poured into the renovation. Every detail had been carefully thought out, creating a space that felt both familiar and new.

As he finished the final touches in the garden, Aunt Kim arrived to see the results of his labor. "Liam, this place looks incredible," she said, her voice filled with admiration. "You've done a remarkable job."

Liam smiled, feeling a deep sense of pride. "Thank you, Aunt Kim. It was a lot of hard work, but it was worth it. This villa means so much to our family, and I'm glad I could restore it."

Aunt Kim nodded, her eyes glistening with emotion. "You've not only restored the villa but also found a new sense of purpose and direction. I'm so proud of you, Liam."

Liam's thoughts drifted to Elara, and he felt a pang of longing. "This villa is a symbol of everything I've worked for, but it's also a reminder of the love I've found. I can't wait for Elara to see it."

Aunt Kim placed a comforting hand on his shoulder. "She'll be here soon enough, and when she sees what you've accomplished, she'll be so proud of you too."

As the day came to a close, Liam sat on the veranda, watching the sun set over the ocean. The colors of the sky mirrored the vibrant hues of the villa, and he felt a deep sense of peace and fulfillment. The renovation was nearly complete, and with it, a chapter of his life had come to an end, paving the way for new beginnings.

Liam pulled out his phone and sent a message to Elara. "The villa is almost finished, Ellie. It's everything we dreamed it would be. I can't wait to show you."

Elara's reply came quickly, filling him with warmth. "I'm so proud of you, Liam. I can't wait to see it and to be with you again. Our journey is just beginning."

With the villa nearly complete, Liam felt ready to face whatever challenges lay ahead. He knew that the bond he shared with Elara would guide him, giving him the strength and courage to pursue his dreams. The island had given him so much—renewed purpose, cherished memories, and a love that would last a lifetime.

As he watched the final rays of sunlight disappear below the horizon, Liam took a deep breath, feeling a sense of contentment and hope. The future was filled with endless possibilities, and he was ready to embrace them, knowing that Elara's love would always be with him.

With the villa renovation complete, Liam felt a deep sense of accomplishment. The island had given him so much—renewed purpose, cherished memories, and a love that would last a lifetime. Now, it was time to face the next challenge: proving himself to his father and reclaiming his place in the family business.

As he packed his bags and prepared to leave the island, Liam felt a mix of excitement and determination. The villa stood as a testament to his hard work and dedication, and he was ready to bring that same energy and passion to the company.

Aunt Kim came to see him off, her eyes filled with pride and emotion. "You've done an incredible job here, Liam," she said, her voice steady. "Your father will see the man you've become and the value you bring to the company."

Liam hugged her tightly, feeling grateful for her support. "Thank you, Aunt Kim. Your belief in me means everything. I'm ready to show my father that I am what the company needs."

As Liam boarded plane to the states, he took one last look at the island, the place that had changed his life in so many ways. The memories of his time with Elara and the hard work he had put into the villa filled him with a sense of pride and determination.

The journey back to the states was a time of reflection for Liam. He thought about the challenges he had faced and overcome, the love he had found, and the man he had become. He knew that the road ahead would not be easy, but he was ready to face it with courage and conviction.

Upon arriving home, Liam headed straight to the family business. He walked into the office, a mix of nerves and determination swirling within him. His father looked up from his desk, surprise evident in his eyes.

"Liam, you're back," his father said, his tone neutral but curious.

Liam nodded, meeting his father's gaze with unwavering confidence. "Yes, Dad. I'm back, and I'm ready to take back control of Blue Peak Construction—the company you entrusted to me before sending me to Isla del Sol. I've learned a lot and grown as a person. I'm committed to making this company succeed, and I want you to enjoy your well-deserved retirement."

His father studied him for a moment before nodding. "Welcome back, son. There's been a lot that transpired while you were in Isla del Sol. Why don't we talk about it tomorrow morning?"

Liam looked at his father for a moment, bewildered at why he was not giving him the accolades to take the company back. "Sure, Dad. No problem. What's another day of you running Blue Peak Construction," he snapped.

His father was taken aback by his son's tone. In all his years he had never heard Liam snap at him. "Son, this is not about me taking the reins."

Liam looked at his father, not quite sure he believed him. "I don't know, Dad, are you sure about that? I mean, you were quick to send me to work on a villa in Isla del Sol without so much as asking me, but telling me, 'Here's your ticket, now go!' Aunt Kim told me she advised you to ask me to come, not command me, but you chose to ignore her advice."

His father sighed, realizing the gravity of his actions. "Liam, the decision to send you to Isla del Sol was not made lightly. I wanted you to gain experience, to see the world and understand the business from a different perspective. It wasn't about sidelining you, but about preparing you for the complexities of running Blue Peak Construction. You know my motto: **Family first. Family above all else. Family supports family.** I did this for our family's future."

Liam shook his head, his frustration evident. "But Dad, you didn't even ask for my input. It felt like a command, not a discussion. How am I supposed to feel ready when I wasn't even part of the decision-making process? If family supports family, why didn't you support my involvement in the decision?"

His father softened, seeing the pain in Liam's eyes. "I see your point, son. Perhaps I was too focused on the end goal and not enough on the journey we were taking together. Let's sit down tomorrow and talk through everything. I want us to be on the same page moving forward because at the end of the day, it's about our family's legacy and working together."

The next morning, Liam arrived at the office early, determined to have a constructive conversation with his father. As he walked in, he noticed his father already seated at the conference table, a cup of coffee in hand.

"Liam, come in," his father said, motioning to the chair across from him.

Liam sat down, feeling a mix of anticipation and apprehension. "Morning, Dad."

"Morning, son. I've been thinking a lot about what you said yesterday. You're right—I should have involved you in the decision. I apologize for that."

Liam nodded, appreciating the acknowledgment. "Thanks, Dad. I just want us to work together and make this company the best it can be. I have some ideas I'd like to discuss."

His father smiled, a hint of pride in his eyes. "I'd like to hear them. But first, I want to explain my reasoning. Sending you to Isla del Sol was about giving you a unique experience, one that I hoped would broaden your perspective and skills. I realize now that I should have trusted you with more responsibility here as well."

Liam leaned forward, his determination evident. "I understand that now. And I did learn a lot from that experience. I want to bring those lessons back to Blue Peak Construction and help us grow. I believe we can do great things together."

His father nodded. "I believe that too. Let's start fresh and move forward as a team, honoring our motto: *Family first. Family above all else. Family supports family.*"

They spent the next few hours discussing their visions for the company, sharing ideas, and planning for the future. It was a meeting filled with respect, understanding, and a renewed sense of partnership.

As the conversation drew to a close, Liam looked at his father thoughtfully. "Dad, I've been thinking about your retirement. You deserve to enjoy your life after all the hard work you've put into the company."

His father sighed, a mix of relief and uncertainty in his expression. "I've been thinking about that too, son. But to be honest, since your mother passed away, the thought of retirement feels daunting. Being alone without her... it's hard to imagine."

Liam felt a pang of sadness for his father. "I understand, Dad. But you don't have to go through it alone. We can figure out ways for you to stay involved with the company, even in a smaller role, if that helps. And you have the rest of the family and me here to support you."

His father reached across the table, placing a hand on Liam's shoulder. "Thank you, Liam. I appreciate that. We'll work together to ensure a smooth transition. Family first, always."

After the meeting, Liam felt a mix of relief and optimism. He pulled out his phone and sent a text to Elara:

> **Liam:** *Hey Elara, just had a really good talk with my dad about the company and his retirement. It felt great to finally clear the air and plan for the future together. I miss you so much. Can't wait to see you soon.*

Chapter 12: A New Vision

Elara and Liam's bond grew stronger with each phone call, their connection unwavering despite the five-hour distance. As Liam poured his efforts into transforming Blue Peak Construction, his vision for the company's future became clear. On the day he finally sat down with his father, his confidence was palpable.

"Dad," Liam began, "I'm fully committed to making Blue Peak Construction thrive. My time on the island and working on the villa taught me the true meaning of hard work and perseverance. I see Blue Peak not just as a luxury home builder, but as a creator of luxury offices that foster a sense of family in every project."

Liam's father raised an eyebrow, a mixture of surprise and curiosity flickering in his eyes. "That's quite a vision, Liam," he said, leaning back in his chair. "I didn't realize you had such ambitious plans. Tell me more about how you intend to achieve this."

Liam gestured around his office, a testament to his meticulous nature and his vision for Blue Peak Construction. The space was modern yet warm, reflecting the company's ethos of blending luxury with a sense of home.

As his father took in the surroundings, he couldn't help but notice the large, mahogany desk that dominated the center of the room. It was polished to a deep shine, with intricate carvings along its edges—a nod to craftsmanship and attention to detail. On the desk, there were neatly organized files, a sleek laptop, and a framed photograph of Liam and Elara from their island retreat. This photo served as a constant reminder of why he was doing this and his hopes for their future together.

Behind the desk, a wall of floor-to-ceiling bookshelves stretched up to the ceiling, filled with architectural books, design magazines, and a few awards Blue Peak Construction had garnered over the years. The shelves were not just for show; they reflected Liam's dedication to continuous learning and excellence.

To the right, large windows allowed natural light to flood the room, offering a panoramic view of the city skyline. The windows were framed by heavy, deep blue curtains that could be drawn for privacy or ambiance.

On the left, a comfortable seating area invited guests to sit and discuss projects. The leather armchairs, paired with a glass coffee table, created an atmosphere of relaxed sophistication. A few architectural models of Blue Peak's projects were displayed on the table, showcasing their innovative designs.

The walls were adorned with framed blueprints and photographs of past projects, each one telling a story of hard work, creativity, and success. There was also a whiteboard with sketches and notes, indicating that Liam often used this space for brainstorming and planning.

The office was immaculate, every element in its place, yet it exuded a sense of warmth and personal touch. It was a space where Liam's professional aspirations and personal growth intersected, making it the perfect environment for shaping the future of Blue Peak Construction.

As Liam continued to outline his strategy, his father listened intently. "One of my key initiatives is to create a website that showcases our hard work. We'll feature photos taken on the jobs, with before-and-after shots to highlight our craftsmanship. This will not only attract potential clients but also instill pride in our team."

Meanwhile, five hours away, Elara was deeply engrossed in her master's classes and perfecting her photography portfolio. Her collection boasted numerous impressive photos, and she was meticulously selecting the best ones when she received an unexpected call from Professor Hayes' office.

Her heart raced as she walked down the hallway, her mind spinning with thoughts. What could this be about? Had she made a mistake? The hallway felt longer than usual, the distant murmur of students adding to her anxiety. The fluorescent lights overhead buzzed softly, casting a stark glow on the polished floors.

As she entered the office, her palms were slightly sweaty, and she took a deep breath to calm herself. The room was filled with shelves of books and framed photographs, a testament to Professor Hayes' own impressive career. A soft light filtered through the blinds, creating a warm, inviting atmosphere despite Elara's nerves.

"Ms. Davis, Elara... please, have a seat," Professor Hayes said, a warm smile on his face. Despite his kind demeanor, Elara couldn't shake off her nerves. She sat down, her stomach in knots, her mind racing through every possible scenario.

"I want to congratulate you on the outstanding photography you've accomplished since our last meeting. I must admit, I was wrong about your work lacking depth and feeling. You've truly captured something special."

Elara's eyes widened in surprise and relief. She could hardly believe the words she was hearing. "Thank you, Professor Hayes. Your feedback made me realize I needed to reflect on my work. I took some time off for a vacation, and it helped me understand what you were trying to tell me. I focused on capturing emotions and stories in my photos."

As she spoke, Elara felt a newfound confidence growing within her. The doubt that had once plagued her was beginning to fade, replaced by a sense of accomplishment and purpose. Professor Hayes nodded, clearly impressed. "It shows, Elara. Keep up the excellent work." Smiling now, Professor Hayes added, "And Elara, if you need help in choosing some photographs for a portfolio I would be honored to help you."

Elara's heart swelled with gratitude. "I would love that, thank you, Professor Hayes," she replied, her voice steady and sincere. As she left the office, she felt lighter, as if a weight had been lifted from her shoulders. The hallway no longer seemed intimidating; instead, it felt like a path leading her to new opportunities and growth.

Later that day, Liam gathered his team in the conference room. The room was spacious, with a large wooden table at its center and a whiteboard on one wall. The atmosphere buzzed with anticipation as the team members settled into their seats, eager to hear what Liam had to share.

Liam stood at the head of the table, projecting confidence and enthusiasm. "Thank you all for coming," he began, looking around at his team. "I've been thinking a lot about how we can take Blue Peak Construction to the next level. One of the key initiatives I want us to focus on is creating a new website."

He paused for a moment, letting the idea sink in. "This website will be more than just a digital business card. I want it to showcase our hard work and craftsmanship, with photos taken on the jobs, including before-and-after shots to highlight the transformations we achieve. It will not only attract potential clients but also instill pride in our team."

Sarah, the company's marketing manager, nodded in agreement. "That's a great idea, Liam. A well-designed website can really make a difference in how clients perceive us. We can also include testimonials and project case studies to build credibility."

Liam smiled, appreciating the support. "Exactly. I envision a section dedicated to client testimonials, where they can share their experiences working with us. And I'd like to have a blog where we can post updates about ongoing projects, industry trends, and insights from our team members."

Tom, the project manager, raised his hand. "How about adding a section that highlights our team's expertise? We could have profiles of key team members with their backgrounds and specialties. It would show clients that we have a skilled and dedicated workforce."

"Great idea, Tom," Liam said, writing it down on the whiteboard. "We want to convey not just the quality of our work, but also the people behind it. Our team is what makes Blue Peak Construction special, and we should highlight that."

Emily, the company's graphic designer, chimed in. "I can start working on some design concepts for the website. We should aim for a clean, modern look that reflects our brand values. We can use high-quality images and consistent branding elements throughout."

"Perfect," Liam replied. "Let's also think about the user experience. The website should be easy to navigate, with clear calls to action so potential clients know how to get in touch with us or request a consultation."

As the team continued to brainstorm, Sarah spoke up again. "Liam, where should we get the photos for the website? Should we take them ourselves or hire a professional photographer?"

Liam considered the question for a moment, a thoughtful look on his face. "That's a great question, Sarah. I have an idea of where we can get them, but I need to check first. I'll follow up on this and get back to everyone with more details soon."

The team nodded in agreement, recognizing the importance of high-quality, professional photos for their new website.

As the meeting progressed, the whiteboard filled with ideas and sketches. The energy in the room was contagious, with everyone contributing their thoughts and expertise. By the end of the meeting, they had a clear plan and a shared vision for the new website.

Liam felt a surge of pride and excitement. This was just the beginning, but he knew that with the support and dedication of his team, Blue Peak Construction was on its way to achieving great things.

Liam quickly pulled out his phone and sent a message to Elara.

"Hey, I have an exciting project for you! We're launching a new website for Blue Peak and I need your amazing photography skills to capture our projects. Can we schedule a photo shoot soon? 😊 Also, could you bring those candid photos of me working on the villa? I'd love to show the team. Can't wait to see you! 😊"

A few moments later, Elara's phone buzzed. She read Liam's message and a big smile spread across her face. She quickly replied:

"That sounds incredible! I'd love to help. Let's plan a time to meet and discuss the details. 😊 And of course, I'll bring the candid photos. Can't wait to see you and miss you tons! ❤"

Liam felt a warmth in his chest as he read her reply. He couldn't wait to see Elara and work together on this exciting new project.

Chapter 13: Hidden Talents

A few days had passed since the team meeting, and Liam could hardly contain his excitement. Today was the day Elara was coming up to spend a couple of days with him, and he couldn't wait to see her.

The office buzzed with the usual activity, but Liam's mind was elsewhere. He glanced at the clock every few minutes, his anticipation growing with each passing second. He had made sure everything was in order for Elara's arrival, planning a few special activities to make her visit memorable.

By mid-afternoon, Liam decided it was time to wrap things up early. He gathered his things and headed to his father's office to say goodbye.

"Hey, Dad," Liam said, peeking through the doorway. "I'm heading out early today. Elara's coming up, and I want to make sure everything's ready for her visit."

Liam's father looked up from his desk, a hint of curiosity in his eyes. "Elara, huh? You've mentioned her a few times. Is she someone special?"

Liam felt a slight blush rise to his cheeks. "Yeah, Dad. She's... she's pretty special to me."

His father raised an eyebrow but didn't press further. "Well, enjoy your time with her, Liam. You've been working hard, and you deserve a break."

"Thanks, Dad. I'll see you tomorrow," Liam replied, his excitement evident in his voice. He quickly made his way out of the office, his heart racing with anticipation.

As Liam's father watched him leave, a smile spread across his face. He shook his head, reminiscing about the early days of his own relationship with Liam's mother. The excitement, the nervousness, and the joy of discovering someone special—all those memories flooded back, bringing a warmth to his heart especially knowing that his son might've found that someone special.

As Liam stepped outside, the crisp air felt invigorating. He took a deep breath, a smile spreading across his face. Today was going to be a special day.

Liam drove home, his mind filled with thoughts of Elara and the wonderful time they would spend together. He couldn't wait to see her smile, hear her laugh, and share his plans for Blue Peak Construction with her.

When he arrived home, he quickly tidied up and prepared a few final touches to make sure everything was perfect for her arrival. As he finished setting up, his phone buzzed with a message from Elara.

"Just left, can't wait to see you! 😊❤"

A few hours later, as the sun began to set, Liam stood by the window, watching the driveway eagerly. Soon, he saw a familiar car pull up. His heart raced as he went outside to greet her.

Elara stepped out of the car, looking a bit tired from the long drive, but her eyes lit up when she saw Liam. They both broke into wide smiles. Liam walked up to her and, without a second thought, pulled her into a warm embrace. They held each other tightly for a moment before Liam gently lifted her chin and kissed her softly.

"Hey," Elara said softly, looking up at him.

"Hey," Liam replied, his voice filled with emotion. "I've missed you so much."

"I've missed you too," Elara said, leaning into the hug, savoring the moment.

They stood there for a few moments, just holding each other, before finally pulling apart. Liam took her hand and asked, "How was the drive?"

"Long, but worth it," Elara replied with a smile. "I'm so happy to be here."

Hand in hand, they walked inside, excited to spend the next few days together. As they entered the house, the delicious aroma of dinner greeted them.

Liam led Elara into the dining room, where the table was set with candles and flowers. "I made us a special dinner," Liam said, his eyes twinkling. "It's inspired by our time on Isla del Sol."

Elara's face lit up with joy. "You did? That's amazing, Liam!"

They sat down to a beautifully prepared meal that brought back memories of their island retreat. The flavors and scents transported them back to the warm, breezy nights they had spent together, and they couldn't help but smile as they reminisced.

"This is perfect," Elara said, taking a bite. "You really know how to surprise me."

Liam reached across the table and took her hand. "I'm glad you like it. I wanted to make this visit special for you."

As they enjoyed their meal, they talked and laughed, feeling closer than ever. The evening was filled with love and happiness, a beautiful reminder of the bond they shared.

Later that night, they found themselves lying together on the couch, wrapped in each other's arms. The room was dimly lit, and the soft hum of the city outside created a peaceful backdrop. Elara snuggled closer to Liam, resting her head on his chest. The pendant Liam had given her still hung around her neck, catching the faint light and reminding them both of that special moment.

Liam gently stroked her hair, his heart full of contentment. "You know," he whispered, "having you here makes everything feel right again."

Elara looked up at him, her eyes reflecting the same sentiment. "I feel the same way. Being with you... it's like everything falls into place."

They lay there in comfortable silence, savoring the warmth and closeness. In each other's arms, they felt a sense of completeness and peace, knowing that no matter what challenges lay ahead, they had each other. And for that moment, everything was perfect.

The next morning, Liam woke up early, eager to show Elara the Blue Peak office. He gently kissed her awake, a soft smile on his face. "Good morning, beautiful. Ready to see where all the magic happens?"
Elara stretched and smiled back. "Good morning. I can't wait."
They got ready and headed to the office together. As they arrived, the team was already bustling with activity. Liam introduced Elara to everyone, and they welcomed her warmly.
"Everyone, this is Elara," Liam said, beaming with pride. "She's here to help us with the photography for our new website."
The team greeted her enthusiastically, and Liam led her on a tour of the office, showing her the different departments and introducing her to key team members.
Finally, they arrived at the conference room, where Liam had set up a presentation to share his vision for the website. The team gathered around, eager to hear Elara's insights and ideas.
"Elara, I thought it would be great for you to share some of your work, especially those candid photos you took of me working on the villa," Liam said, looking at her with admiration.
Elara nodded, feeling a mix of excitement and nerves. She connected her laptop to the projector and began showcasing her photos. The team watched in awe as they saw the beautiful, heartfelt moments Elara had captured.
"These are incredible," Sarah, the marketing manager, said. "You have an amazing talent, Elara."
"Thank you," Elara replied, feeling grateful for the warm reception. "I'm really excited to work with all of you on this project."
Liam squeezed her hand, his heart swelling with pride. "Elara will be visiting some of our job sites and taking photos of the team in action, as well as capturing the essence of what makes Blue Peak Construction special—our people."
Elara's eyes sparkled with enthusiasm. "I'm so excited to get started. I can't wait to meet everyone and capture the amazing work you all do."

Over the next few days, Elara visited various job sites, capturing candid shots of the team members hard at work. She photographed the construction process, the intricate details of the projects, and the camaraderie among the team. Each photo told a story, highlighting the dedication and passion that drove the Blue Peak team.

Elara also spent time at the office, taking portraits of the personnel who made the company run smoothly. From the architects and designers to the project managers and support staff, she captured their personalities and the unique contributions they brought to the company.

As Elara reviewed the photos, she felt a deep sense of fulfillment. She knew that these images would showcase the heart and soul of Blue Peak Construction, helping to create a website that truly reflected the company's values and vision.

One afternoon, as Elara was editing photos in the office, Pete walked in. He smiled warmly at her. "Elara, it's so nice to finally meet you. Liam's told me a lot about you."

Elara stood up and shook his hand. "It's wonderful to meet you too, Mr. Greyson. Thank you for having me here."

"Please, call me Pete," he said, his eyes twinkling with kindness. "I've been very impressed with the photos I've seen so far. You have a real talent."

"Thank you, Pete," Elara replied, feeling a mix of gratitude and nervousness.

Just then, Liam walked in, beaming at the sight of his dad and Elara getting along. "Hey, Dad. I was thinking, how about we all go out for dinner tonight? Elara's been working so hard, and I think it would be nice to relax and celebrate a bit."

Pete nodded in agreement. "That's a great idea, Liam. Actually, I'll invite your brother Ethan too. He's been wanting to catch up with you."

Liam's eyes lit up. "That sounds perfect. Elara, you'll love Ethan. He's a doctor and always has some interesting stories to share."

Elara smiled. "I'd love to meet him."

That evening, they all gathered at a cozy restaurant in town. The atmosphere was warm and inviting, with soft music playing in the background. Ethan joined them, and they all shared stories, laughter, and good food.

Chapter 14: Shared Moments

That evening, they all gathered at "La Bella Vita," a cozy Italian restaurant known for its charming ambiance and delectable cuisine. The soft glow of candlelight and the soothing melodies of a jazz pianist set the perfect backdrop for their dinner.

Liam, Elara, Pete, and Ethan were seated at a corner table adorned with a beautiful floral arrangement. The scent of freshly baked bread and rich marinara filled the air.

Liam raised his glass. "To family, friends, and new beginnings," he toasted.

Everyone clinked their glasses together with smiles all around.

Ethan leaned in, his eyes twinkling with curiosity. "So, Elara, Liam's told me you're a talented photographer. I'd love to hear more about your work and what drew you to photography."

Elara smiled, feeling warmly welcomed by Liam's family. "Thank you, Ethan. I've always been drawn to capturing moments that tell a story. Photography allows me to preserve emotions and memories in a way that words sometimes can't. My master's program has been a challenging but rewarding journey, and I'm grateful for the opportunity to grow as an artist."

Pete nodded appreciatively. "Your photos for Blue Peak are exceptional. They truly capture the spirit of our team and the hard work that goes into each project."

"Thank you, Pete," Elara replied, feeling a mix of pride and gratitude. "Working with Liam and the team has been an incredible experience. It's inspiring to see the passion and dedication everyone brings to their work."

Pete leaned forward; his eyes filled with excitement. "I can't wait to see the new website with your photos, Elara. I believe they'll enhance our online presence significantly and show the world what Blue Peak Construction is all about."

Elara beamed at the encouragement. "I'm really excited to see it all come together. It's been a wonderful collaboration, and I hope the website truly reflects the heart and soul of Blue Peak."

As the evening continued, they shared stories and laughter. Ethan recounted amusing anecdotes from his medical practice, and Pete reminisced about his early days in the construction industry. Elara felt a deep sense of belonging, as if she had known Liam's family for much longer than just a few days.

The conversation eventually turned to Liam and Elara's relationship. Ethan looked at Liam with a playful grin. "So, Liam, how did you and Elara meet?"

Liam chuckled, glancing at Elara before answering. "We met on vacation in Isla del Sol. It was one of those chance encounters that felt like fate. We connected instantly and decided to continue our relationship long-distance. It's been challenging at times, but it's also made us stronger."

Pete nodded thoughtfully. "Elara, where are you attending for your master's program?"

"I'm attending Seabrook University," Elara replied. "It's been an amazing experience, and I'm learning so much. The faculty and facilities there are top-notch."

Ethan smiled. "That's fantastic. Seabrook is a great school. It must be challenging to balance your studies and a long-distance relationship."

Elara nodded. "It can be tough, but Liam and I make it work. We support each other, and that makes all the difference."

Pete raised his glass again. "To Liam and Elara, and to all the wonderful moments ahead."

As they toasted once more, Pete's eyes twinkled with a hint of excitement. "By the way, Elara, while Liam was away, I put in a bid for a project at Seabrook University. We just heard back from them, and it looks like we might get to work on the new Art Gallery!"

Elara's eyes widened in surprise and delight. "Wow, that's amazing! The Art Gallery is going to be a fantastic project. I'm so excited for you, Pete!"

Liam looked at his father with a mix of surprise and pride. "Dad, that's incredible news. Working on the Art Gallery at Seabrook will be a great opportunity for Blue Peak."

Pete smiled warmly. "I thought it would be a wonderful way to strengthen our connection with the university, and who knows, maybe Elara can be involved in the project too."

Elara's heart swelled with gratitude. "Thank you, Pete. I would love to contribute in any way I can."

As the dinner continued, they discussed the exciting possibilities of the new project and how it could bring them all closer together. Elara felt a deep sense of gratitude for the love and support that surrounded her. She knew that no matter where life took her, she had found something truly special with Liam and his family.

After a delightful dinner filled with laughter, stories, and exciting news, Liam and Elara said their goodbyes to Pete and Ethan. They walked hand-in-hand to the car, the crisp evening air wrapping around them like a cozy blanket.

As they drove back to Liam's place, the city lights blurred into a beautiful mosaic through the car windows. The comfortable silence between them was punctuated by the soft hum of the engine.

Liam glanced at Elara, a warm smile spreading across his face. "Tonight was wonderful. I loved seeing you connect with my family."

Elara returned the smile, her heart full. "Your family is amazing, Liam. I feel so welcomed and loved."

When they arrived at Liam's home, they walked inside, kicking off their shoes and settling into the living room. Liam turned on a few soft lamps, casting a gentle glow around the room. They sank into the couch, Elara leaning her head on Liam's shoulder.

"I can't believe my dad put in a bid at Seabrook for the Art Gallery," Liam said, breaking the comfortable silence. "It's such an incredible opportunity."

Elara nodded, her eyes reflecting her excitement. "It really is. Imagine working on a project that's so close to my heart and my school. It's like everything is aligning perfectly."

Liam gently took her hand, his thumb tracing small circles on her palm. "I think it's a sign, Elara. We're meant to be together, supporting each other in our dreams and careers."

Elara's heart swelled with emotion. "I feel the same way. Knowing that Blue Peak will be working on the Art Gallery while I'm finishing my master's program is like having the best of both worlds."

They sat in silence for a moment, savoring the closeness and the shared dreams. Liam looked into Elara's eyes; his voice filled with sincerity. "Elara, I've been thinking a lot about our future. I want us to be together, to build a life where we support each other and grow together."

Elara squeezed his hand, her eyes shining with love. "I want that too, Liam. Being with you makes everything feel right. I believe we can make it work, no matter the distance or the challenges."

Liam smiled, feeling a deep sense of contentment. "We'll figure it out, one step at a time. And who knows, maybe in the near future, we'll be working on projects together more often."

Elara snuggled closer, resting her head on his chest. "I can't wait for that. Until then, we'll cherish every moment we have together and make the most of our time apart."

As they lay there, wrapped in each other's arms, the future seemed bright and full of possibilities. They knew that no matter what challenges lay ahead, they had each other, and that made everything perfect.

The next morning, sunlight streamed through the curtains, gently waking Liam and Elara. They shared a peaceful moment, savoring the warmth of each other's presence before starting the day.

After a quick breakfast, they made their way to the Blue Peak office. The anticipation in the air was palpable as the team prepared for the official launch of the new website.

Liam held Elara's hand as they walked into the office, greeted by smiles and nods from the team. Sarah, the marketing manager, approached them with a grin. "Today's the big day! Ready to see the fruits of our labor?"

Elara nodded enthusiastically. "I can't wait. It's been such a collaborative effort, and I'm excited to see how it all comes together."

The team gathered in the conference room, where a large screen displayed the new Blue Peak Construction website. Liam stepped forward, addressing the room. "Everyone, thank you for your hard work and dedication. Today, we unveil our new website, which showcases not only our projects but also the amazing people behind them."

With a click, the website went live, and the room filled with applause and cheers. The homepage featured a stunning slideshow of Elara's photographs, capturing the essence of Blue Peak's work and the team's camaraderie.

Sarah guided them through the various sections of the website, highlighting the projects, team profiles, and the new blog featuring behind-the-scenes stories. The team was thrilled, and the positive energy in the room was infectious.

Pete approached Elara with a proud smile. "Your photos have truly transformed our online presence, Elara. We're already receiving fantastic feedback from clients and partners."

Elara felt a swell of pride and gratitude. "Thank you, Pete. I'm honored to have been a part of this project. It's been an incredible experience."

Liam stood by her side; his eyes filled with admiration. "This is just the beginning, Elara. Together, we can achieve so much more."

As the celebration continued, Elara and Liam shared a quiet moment, reflecting on the journey that had brought them here. The launch of the website marked a significant milestone in their lives, both personally and professionally.

Later that day, as they returned to Liam's place, they talked about their future plans. Sitting together on the couch, Liam looked into Elara's eyes, his voice filled with determination. "Elara, I want us to build a life where we can support each other's dreams and be together, no matter what."

Elara smiled, her heart full. "I believe we can do that, Liam. With Blue Peak working on the Art Gallery at Seabrook, it feels like everything is aligning perfectly. We'll make it work, one step at a time."

As the evening grew darker, and the hum of the city softened, Liam found himself lying awake, his thoughts racing. He replayed the events of the past few days, feeling a deep sense of gratitude and excitement.

He glanced over at Elara, peacefully asleep beside him. She had brought so much joy and light into his life, and he couldn't imagine a future without her. The news about the Art Gallery project felt like a sign, a confirmation that they were on the right path.

In the quiet of the night, Liam made a silent vow. No matter the distance or the challenges, he would do everything in his power to make their dreams come true. Together, they were unstoppable. They were more than friends; they were partners in life, supporting each other through thick and thin.

Meanwhile, Elara stirred slightly, her thoughts mirroring Liam's. She marveled at how their paths had intertwined so seamlessly, despite the miles that often separated them. Liam's unwavering support and belief in her had been her anchor. She knew that their bond went beyond mere friendship—it was a partnership built on love, trust, and a shared vision for the future.

She reflected on the significance of the Art Gallery project at Seabrook. It was not just a professional opportunity but a symbol of their interconnected lives. Working on the project would allow them to blend their worlds, creating something beautiful and lasting together.

Elara smiled softly, feeling a profound sense of peace. She knew that whatever challenges lay ahead, they would face them together, as partners. Liam's dreams had become hers, and her aspirations were now a shared goal.

As they lay there, lost in their reflections, they both understood that their relationship was more than a coincidence. It was a deliberate choice, a commitment to supporting each other's dreams and building a life together. They were partners in every sense of the word, ready to take on the world, hand in hand.

The future seemed bright and full of possibilities. With their love, support, and shared dreams, they knew they were meant to be together. And that thought carried them both into a peaceful sleep, dreaming of the many adventures yet to come.

Chapter 15: A New Dawn

One Year Later

The auditorium at Seabrook University buzzed with excitement as families and friends gathered to celebrate the graduating class. The stage was adorned with flowers, and the air was filled with the sound of joyous chatter and laughter.

Liam sat in the front row, his heart swelling with pride as he scanned the sea of graduates. His eyes were fixed on Elara, who stood among her classmates, her smile radiant and her eyes sparkling with accomplishment.

Over the past year, their bond had only grown stronger. They had navigated the challenges of long-distance with grace and resilience, their love unwavering. Liam had made frequent trips to Seabrook, and Elara had become an integral part of the Blue Peak team, contributing her creative talents to the Art Gallery project and other ventures.

As Elara's name was called, Liam felt a surge of emotion. He watched with admiration as she walked across the stage, accepting her diploma with grace and pride. She had worked so hard to achieve this milestone, and he couldn't be prouder.

When the ceremony concluded, Liam made his way through the crowd, searching for Elara. He found her surrounded by friends and family, all offering their congratulations. When their eyes met, Elara's face lit up, and she ran to him, throwing her arms around his neck.

"You did it, Elara," Liam whispered, holding her close. "I'm so proud of you."

Elara pulled back slightly, looking into his eyes. "Thank you, Liam. I couldn't have done it without your support. You mean everything to me."

Liam smiled, his heart full. "And you mean everything to me. Now, let's celebrate this incredible achievement together."

They spent the rest of the day celebrating with friends and family. As the evening approached, they gathered at a charming rooftop restaurant, the city lights twinkling around them. The warm breeze carried the scent of blooming flowers, adding to the magical atmosphere.

As they enjoyed their meal, Liam excused himself for a moment. He returned with a surprised smile and guided Elara to the edge of the rooftop, where a familiar face awaited them.

"I have a special visitor for you," Liam said, his voice filled with excitement. "Aunt Kim wanted to be here for this special moment."

Elara's eyes widened in surprise and delight. "Aunt Kim! It's so wonderful to see you again!"

Aunt Kim smiled warmly, pulling Elara into a hug. "I've heard so much about your achievements, Elara. I'm thrilled to be here to celebrate with you. And it's wonderful to see the two of you together, happy and thriving."

As they chatted, the sun began to set, casting a golden glow over the city. Liam took Elara's hand and led her to a quieter spot on the rooftop, away from the others.

"Elara, there's something I've been wanting to say," Liam began, his heart pounding with anticipation. "Over the past year, we've faced challenges, celebrated successes, and grown closer than ever. You've become my partner, my confidante, and my inspiration."

He reached into his pocket and pulled out a small velvet box, opening it to reveal a beautiful engagement ring. "Elara, I can't imagine my life without you. Will you marry me and be my partner for life?"

Tears welled up in Elara's eyes as she looked at Liam, her heart overflowing with love. "Yes, Liam, yes! I want to spend the rest of my life with you."

Liam slipped the ring onto her finger, and they embraced, their hearts beating in perfect harmony. As they returned to their family and friends, cheers and congratulations filled the air.

Aunt Kim hugged them both tightly. "I knew from the moment you two met at the villa that you were meant to be together. I'm so happy for you both."

The future seemed brighter than ever, filled with love, support, and endless possibilities. With their love, support, and shared dreams, they knew they were meant to be together. And that thought carried them both into a new chapter of their lives, ready to face whatever adventures lay ahead, hand in hand.

Epilogue

The sun dipped below the horizon, casting a warm, golden glow over the Azure Cove villa on Isla del Sol. The soft sound of waves crashing against the shore created a serene melody, and the gentle breeze rustled the palm leaves, adding to the tranquil atmosphere.

Liam and Elara stood hand-in-hand on the balcony, gazing out at the breathtaking view. The past year had been a whirlwind of emotions, challenges, and triumphs, culminating in a beautiful wedding that celebrated their love and commitment to each other.

Now, as they basked in the warmth of the setting sun, they felt a profound sense of contentment and joy. Their honeymoon in Isla del Sol and staying in the Azures Seas villa was a perfect blend of nostalgia and new beginnings. It was here, in this idyllic paradise, that their journey had begun, and now, it was where they celebrated the start of their life together as husband and wife.

Elara leaned her head on Liam's shoulder, a soft smile playing on her lips. "I can't believe we're back here, Liam. This place holds so many memories for us."

Liam wrapped his arm around her, pulling her closer. "It's like coming full circle, isn't it? From the moment we met, to building our lives together, and now being here as a married couple. It feels like a dream."

Elara looked up at him, her eyes filled with love. "A dream come true. I feel so grateful for everything we've experienced and for the future we have ahead of us."

Liam nodded, his heart swelling with emotion. "Me too, Elara. We've faced so much together, and through it all, we've only grown stronger. I can't wait to see what the future holds for us."

They stood in silence for a few moments, savoring the beauty of the sunset and the promise of their shared life. The villa, with its familiar charm and comforting ambiance, felt like a sanctuary where they could escape the world and focus on each other.

As the stars began to twinkle in the night sky, they made their way to the villa's terrace, where a candlelit dinner awaited them. The table was adorned with fresh flowers and twinkling fairy lights, creating a magical ambiance.

Over dinner, they reminisced about their journey, from their chance meeting on the island to the many milestones they had achieved together. They laughed, shared stories, and celebrated their love, knowing that their bond was unbreakable.

After dinner, they strolled along the beach, the cool sand beneath their feet and the moon casting a silver glow over the water. Elara's pendant, a gift from Liam, glimmered under the moonlight, a symbol of their unbreakable bond. They felt a sense of peace and fulfillment, knowing that they had found their forever in each other.

As they returned to the villa, Liam took Elara's hand and looked into her eyes. "Elara, I promise to love you, support you, and cherish every moment we have together. You are my everything."

Elara smiled, her heart overflowing with love. "And I promise to love you, stand by you, and make every day an adventure. Together, we can conquer anything."

Liam's eyes sparkled with joy. "I can't wait for the day when we bring our children here to Isla del Sol. We'll create new memories together, just like we did when we first met."

Elara's smile widened, her heart swelling with happiness. "I look forward to that too, Liam. Our family will have so many beautiful moments here."

They sealed their vows with a kiss, the gentle waves providing a soothing symphony. As they held each other close, they knew that their love story was just beginning, and the best was yet to come.

The Azure Cove villa, with its timeless beauty and cherished memories, was the perfect place to start their new chapter. And as they drifted off to sleep that night, wrapped in each other's arms, they dreamed of the many adventures and beautiful moments that awaited them, knowing that they were meant to be together, forever.

Don't miss out!

Visit the website below and you can sign up to receive emails whenever Stephanie Doering publishes a new book. There's no charge and no obligation.

https://books2read.com/r/B-A-AEBUB-BGAXF

BOOKS 2 READ

Connecting independent readers to independent writers.

Also by Stephanie Doering

Safe Haven
Safe Haven
Naughty Indulgences: The Ultimate Birthday Gift
Veil of Shadows: The Master's Unraveling

The Weeping Ridge Series
The Ghosts of Willowtree Manor

Standalone
The Weekend Getaway
Claiming Her
Club Abyss
Sun Kissed Hearts

Watch for more at https://books2read.com/author/stepjhanie-doering/subscribe/1/809276/.

About the Author

Stephanie Doering was born and raised in Norwalk, CT but now resides in North Carolina with her husband of 18 years and their three teenagers. When she is not busy playing chauffeur to one of her three teenagers you can find Stephanie at home in her office working on her next masterpiece. In her free time she likes to curl up in her favoite chair with a good book to read. She enjoys reading genres such as romance, erotica, paranormal romance and BDSM, all of which you can find her writing about as well.

Read more at https://books2read.com/author/stepjhanie-doering/subscribe/1/809276/.